## The men of EAGLE FORCE

**VIC GABRIEL**—The heart and soul of Eagle Force, Vic is an ex–Special Forces soldier, the son of a Green Beret—and one tough S.O.B. who does not know the meaning of the word compromise. He's happiest when waging the good fight and spitting in the eye of Death.

**JOHNNY SIMMS**—"Johnny-Boy" is a fifth-degree black belt and soldier for hire who lived through torture in a Central American prison. In this bad world gone mad he believes the only way to survive is to be badder and madder than the next dude.

**HENRY van BOOLEWARKE**—"The Dutchman" is actually a Recces commando from South Africa. He thinks nothing of holding off a whole army of Marxist-backed guerrillas with some Molotov cocktails and an HK 33 West German assault rifle.

**ZAC DILLINGER**—Known to his friends as Bad Zac, he's an ex-merc turned private eye whose hero is General Patton. He never goes anywhere without a black leather shoulder holster that holds two pearl-handled Colt .45s.

# CONTRACT FOR SLAUGHTER

## Dan Schmidt

BANTAM BOOKS

NEW YORK · TORONTO · LONDON · SYDNEY · AUCKLAND

*For Ray Puechner,*
*who was right there from the very beginning.*
*His spirit of faith and courage lives on.*
*I can only hope I learned well.*

CONTRACT FOR SLAUGHTER

*A Bantam Book / August 1989*

ISBN 0-553-27637-9

*Published simultaneously in the United States and Canada*

Bantam Books are published by Bantam Books, a division of Bantam
Doubleday Dell Publishing Group, Inc. Its trademark, consisting of
the words "Bantam Books" and the portrayal of a rooster, is
Registered in U.S. Patent and Trademark Office and in other
countries. Marca Registrada. Bantam Books, 666 Fifth Avenue, New
York, New York 10103

PRINTED IN THE UNITED STATES OF AMERICA

O      0 9 8 7 6 5 4 3 2 1

# Chapter 1

The victims of the terrorist attack burned, their charred limbs tangled in a web of roasting flesh. A ring of flames sealed the dead in the fiery charnel house, licking out into the street with raging tongues that threatened to incinerate bystanders. From the slaughter zone, a pall of black smoke swept over the horrified crowd, blotting out the Eiffel Tower in the distance. The walking wounded who had been burned in the attack screamed in agony. Sirens wailed, and more than a dozen ambulances and fire trucks flooded the scene, gendarmes struggling to hold back the swollen pack of onlookers.

> . . . *Because of the horror and shock surrounding this scene of sudden violence, there is no way at the moment to determine how many have perished in this, the latest wave of terrorist attacks in Europe. It is believed that at least eighty people were in the cafe at noon when terrorists, armed with flamethrowers . . .*

He walked out onto the deck of his thirty-five foot houseboat, a ham sandwich in one hand, a bottle of Budweiser in the other hand. He was a big man, six foot three inches tall, his body lean and hard with chiseled muscles, his dark hair closely cropped, combed back from a square-jawed face that looked as if it was carved out of granite. No, he didn't appear to be the kind of man to be taken lightly, either in a verbal or physical confrontation. He would stand out in a crowd. He had experienced intense personal suffering, seen death and horror, and it showed in the haunted pools of his deepset gray-green eyes.

The *Finer Things in Life* now anchored in his private cove in Key Largo, he had just returned from cruising the Gulf of Mexico and hot-footing it up the Atlantic seaboard to escape the hurricane months of August and September. With his return to reality, he was concerned in checking the steel hull for dry rot and peeling paint, taking a look at the underwater fittings, and getting an idea of how much the repair work would dent his Swiss bank account.

Then he saw the carnage on the six o'clock news. And he felt his blood run hot with rage, the blood pressure pounding into his ears.

Reality was there, all right, striking Vic Gabriel in the face, like a bolt of lightning out of the blue sky.

> *. . . this is the eighth such suicide attack in the past month by the terrorist group calling itself* Sadi.*"*

The sun was setting, a blood-red orb suspended in a crimson sky beyond the giant palm trees at the west end of the cove, light dancing off the greenish waters like strands of diamond beads. Pelicans flapped over the water at the end of the dock, skimming the surface in their relentless quest for food. The hunter and the hunted. The living, the dead, and the dying. Even though he was aware of the eternal struggle of life and death around him, this was still his quiet time, the evening peace when the man could relax, gather his thoughts, reflect on the day.

Now this horror on the television stoked the fires of black violence in Vic Gabriel's heart. *Sadi.* Yeah, he thought, there they were on the six o'clock news again.

## Contract for Slaughter

Every night for the past three weeks straight he'd heard that name on television and radio. *Sadi.* The newspeople said *Sadi* meant Sword of Islam. To Vic Gabriel, *Sadi* meant shitsucker. And not only *Sadi.* Whatever his religious or political cause, whatever the color of his skin, anyone who perpetrated this kind of horror against the family of man was an enemy to Vic Gabriel's way of thinking. What he saw on that television screen, the bloody aftermath of more so-called unconventional warfare, made him wish he could drive his fist through that screen at the bastards who had shed so much innocent blood across Europe, grab them by the throat and strangle the life out of them, squeeze their throats until the blood and spittle gushed out of their mouths, crush their necks until their eyeballs popped out of their sockets. Damn, but he wanted to torch those *Sadi* punks with a flamethrower himself. What *Sadi* had done across Europe during the past few weeks was chickenshit stuff. Plain, and very goddamn simple. Chickenshit. Sorrow in his eyes and rage in his heart, he shook his hand, put the beer and sandwich down on the bench. How could he eat or enjoy a cold beer after looking at such a hellish scene? Who would use flamethrowers of all things in a suicide attack against innocent people? Torch human beings as though they were nothing more than garbage to be incinerated?

> *Exactly what is prompting these attacks by the terrorist group calling itself* Sadi, *or, as they wish to be called, the Sword of Islam, is not known. . . .*

Christ, he thought, *not known?* Why not take on somebody who can fight back? Why not . . . God damn it! *Whatever happened to the days,* he wondered, *when two guys who just didn't like each other went out and knocked heads until one was down for good? This senseless butch-*

3

*ering of women and children, the bombs planted in cars, the hijackings . . . fucking gutless barbarism.*

But face-to-face squaring off wasn't the way terrorists operated, he knew from grim experience. Butchers in the shadows, terrorists served only themselves, gave glory to some dark, twisted cause. Terrorists saw themselves as heroes and martyrs, but there was nothing heroic about them or their crimes. They were gutless sacks of shit.

Seething with fury over what he'd seen on television the past few weeks, Vic Gabriel had been wondering what he could do to get back out there in the hellgrounds with his own special brand of cleansing fire. Christ, everywhere he turned, the walls of civilization seemed to be crumbling under the constant deathblows from terrorists and drug-lords and other international scum. An abyss of sudden death and terrible suffering had yawned open to swallow the innocents of the world. The world, he found himself believing, needed his deadly martial skills—again. Besides, he was bored with the fisherman's life; he longed for that adrenaline rush—again.

At one time, years ago, Vic Gabriel had stood at the very edge of the abyss. Looking down. He'd fought back. Raged with the good fight and spat back in the eye of Death and Destruction. Once again, he felt himself being drawn, inexplicably, toward the Fire.

His days as a free-lance CIA assassin and soldier-for-hire were dead and gone. Buried beneath the crushing weight of terrible memories. Memories that haunted his sleep. Memories that taunted him, burned anguish into his soul. Memories that lived like ghosts in the back of his mind. But Vic Gabriel knew what he had to do—what *had* to be done.

For the past month he'd been giving some hard and serious thought to savaging the savages himself. Fighting fire with fire. He had the money—hell, yes. Squirreled away in that Swiss bank account, thanks to the CIA paychecks from his days as a soldier-for-hire. The idea had been burning in his mind for weeks: an elite search-and-destroy team. Manhunters. Savage hunters. He had just the men in mind, and he knew where he'd find at least two of his manhunters off the bat. So what the hell was stopping him from getting the juggernaut in gear? Certainly not time or money, because he had both. Maybe too much of both. Laziness? Uh-uh.

The Fire was back. And it was burning out of control. *Sadi* had unchained the beast in Gabriel's belly. What had the CIA called him so long ago? The Angel of Death. The Apocalypse Soldier. Well, it was time he started living up to those names again. On his own terms. In his own way.

Time to walk back into the Eye of the Fire.

The creaking of wood jarred Gabriel from his grim thoughts. Whirling, he spotted four men in black three-piece suits. They froze at the end of the dock, startled, apparently, by the savage intensity in the lone man's eyes.

In less than a heartbeat, Gabriel's hand snaked beneath the bench and fisted a weapon.

The stainless steel .45 Colt ACP didn't waver a fraction of an inch, as Gabriel trained the barrel on the four strangers. One guy carried a briefcase. The head honcho, Gabriel determined. Any screwing around and that one would be the first to bite the Great Worm.

Whoever they were, the former Company assassin sized them up as trouble. Life had already thrown Vic Gabriel enough trouble, enough grief. Fuck it, he decided. If these clowns had come looking for trouble, Vic Gabriel wasn't about to disappoint them.

5

# Chapter 2

"Just what the hell are you people supposed to be? Pallbearers?"

Cold silence. Behind Gabriel, a newscaster hammered out a special report on international terrorism. His grim attention, though, steeled on his strange, and very likely bad, company, Gabriel glimpsed the lopsided grin on the big dude with the crewcut. Even at a good ten meters' distance, Gabriel spotted the bulges beneath the jackets of the three goons, knew they were packing iron.

"Funny man, huh, Mr. Milton," a short, stocky blond guy grunted. "Sounds like we found the right turkey. . . ."

"Shut up," the man addressed as "Milton" hissed. Milton was a man of medium height, but lean and hard, as though he worked out at a gym daily. He was impeccably dressed in a suit that Gabriel judged to be made of silk. Imported, no doubt. Closely cropped dark hair, not one strand out of place. Black loafers, probably Italian leather, Gabriel thought. That guy had money, and he liked to wear it with flash. The other three men were obviously gorillas, muscle to keep that flash flawless and unsoiled.

"This is private property you've just stepped on, people," Gabriel growled. "I could blow you away, dump you in the water and let you float out to sea and no one would be the wiser."

"You wouldn't do that."

The imported special, Milton, was a little too cool and cocky for Gabriel's liking. "Yeah. Why not?"

"Because you'd lose out on the chance to make a lot of money, that's why. And the chance to get back out there and do what you do best."

"All right, since you seem to think you know what I do best, let's cut the crap. Who are you? What do you want? You've got about five seconds to answer before I start pulling the trigger."

"Now, wait a minute."

"Three seconds."

Silk Suit scowled. "Okay, hard guy. My name is Bradley Milton III, and what we've come here for is precisely to make some funeral arrangements. Can we talk like civilized men? No chilly dialogue. No pointed guns."

"How did you find me?"

"Can we talk?"

Gabriel was suspicious, but his curiosity was aroused. He'd quit the Company after that last aborted fiasco in Libya, where he'd been headhunting for the Colonel himself, and no one, repeat no one, should have known his whereabouts. Unless, of course, these goons standing on his dock were Company SOD operatives themselves. The tentacles of the CIA stretched worldwide. Once bitten by the Special Operations Division, you stayed juiced by its venom—for life. There was no place to run to, nowhere to hide from those people. Vic Gabriel suspected when he quit that he wouldn't be allowed to just walk away from the Company as though he was going home from a Sunday picnic.

If the Company had taken the trouble to find him, what did they want? Blood, most likely.

"Okay," Gabriel decided, "let's unload the hardware first. Real slow. Left hands. One man at a time. Work it from my left to right."

They did as Gabriel ordered. Each man reached inside his jacket, withdrew his firepower, dropped the weapons on the dock. Wood banged with the weight of each fallen gun. Big guns, too. Cannons. All .44 Magnums. Four-, six-, and eight-inch barrels, respectively. Satin stainless steel that glinted for a heartbeat in the dying sunlight. The kind of guns that left gaping wound canals in targets. Milton showed Gabriel that he was unarmed.

"Now, can we talk?"

"The rest of it. Pull up the pants legs. Take off the jackets."

Sure enough, each of the three gorillas had a SIG-Sauer P-230 9mm pistol strapped to his ankle. When they shed their jackets, they also unsheathed stainless steel folded switchblades.

Gabriel's grip tightened around his .45 Colt. "I thought you came to talk?"

"Let me come aboard and explain."

"Why don't you do that. And I'd better like that explanation. Or you'll be on about those funeral arrangements . . . dead on."

Moments later, the four men boarded the *Finer Things in Life*. Gabriel stood on the other side of the Formica table that was secured to the deck of the boathouse. He noticed Milton was holding onto his briefcase so tight that his knuckles were white, stuck out like the edges of razors.

A strange smile creased Milton's face as he listened to the news special on terrorism.

> . . . *laws, both national and international, cannot and will not stop, much less contain, the scourge of terrorism. What, then, can be done to prevent* . . .

Suddenly, Milton snapped off the television set. "Do you believe that everything in life is timing, Mr. Gabriel?"

One of the gorillas rocked the boat gently, swaying back and forth on the balls of his feet. He looked at Gabriel and cracked, "Nice buoyancy."

Gabriel tucked his .45 Colt inside the top of his gray

sweat pants, ignored the gorilla, looked at Milton. "That depends."

"On what?"

"On whose timing. Now, stop dancing with me, pal. Start answering some questions. Have your goons," Gabriel said, injecting ice into his gray-green eyes, "sit down on the bench over there. Hands folded between their legs like they were going to play with themselves."

Milton nodded at his goons, and they sat on the bench opposite Gabriel.

Gabriel took a sip of beer. "Now . . . start talking."

"As I told you, I'm Bradley Milton III, president of Milton Import–Export of San Francisco."

"Just what do you import and export, Brad?" Something wasn't right here. Gabriel smelled a setup.

"It's Mr. Milton, Mr. Gabriel."

"Yeah, sure." Gabriel had never been a man to walk softly. He had always had a smart mouth, considered it a gift for those who knew when and how to use it. Smart mouths were usually the outpourings of a smart mind, the unleashed aggressions and frustrations pent up in a soul wearied and troubled by the world.

"What I import and export is none of your business. If you doubt who I am, it's certainly easy enough to check out."

"I will. Go on," Gabriel said, and fished a pack of Marlboros out of the pocket of his sports shirt. With a gold-plated Zippo, he torched the smoke. On the Zippo was an engraving of a Death's Head. Beneath the Death's Head was inscribed *7th SFG—no compromise*.

"I came to you, Mr. Gabriel, because I was looking for a so-called specialist. A man of action. A man of violence. A man," Milton said, standing before Gabriel and looking pointedly at the Zippo on the table, "of no compromise."

"That doesn't explain how you found me."

"I have my sources."

"Confidential, no doubt."

"No doubt. You see, Mr. Gabriel, I had you checked out for a very good reason." Milton cleared his throat suddenly, glanced at his goons, then asked, "Can we talk inside your cabin?"

"Why? I'm perfectly comfortable out here."

"I would be more comfortable inside, where we can sit and talk in private. There are some details of this visit that not even my own bodyguards know. Things about yourself, also, that you may not want other men to hear. I think you understand, don't you?"

Gabriel drew deeply on his smoke, then took another drink of beer. Whatever Milton was up to, he was making some sense in his own twisted, mysterious way. Hell, it wouldn't hurt, Gabriel figured, to hear the man out. Maybe timing, after all was everything in life. Maybe Milton's timing was more than jut a coincidence?

"All right, Milton, inside. You three," Gabriel told the goons, "sit tight. Keep your balls in your hands."

One of the bodyguards, a bear-sized man with a head as bald as a cue ball, scowled. It was obvious to Gabriel that guy wanted some toe-to-toe action. Gabriel was in the mood to oblige that goon if he got froggy.

Gabriel followed Milton inside the cabin, shut the door behind him. Through a porthole beside the door, Gabriel could keep an eye on Milton's goon squad. Right away, Milton's gaze fell on the mahogany walls. Bookshelves were lined with volumes on exploration and war. Napoleon. Rommel. Frederick the Great. Julius Caesar. The Third Reich. The rise and fall of ancient Rome. The barbarian tribes of the Dark Ages. Columbus. Bartholomeu Dias. Cyrus the Great. The Mongol Empire. Clausewitz. There were works as well by Dante, Camus, Dostoevski, Goethe.

"I'm impressed. Excellent taste in literature. You're a fan of history also, Mr. Gabriel."

"Not a fan. A student."

Milton pursed his lips, as if he was going to apologize. "I see," he mused, then looked at the array of knives and

swords hanging on both sides of a mural of the Grande
Armée's retreat across the corpse-littered, bloodstained,
snow-blanketed steppe of Russia. "What are these?"

"Souvenirs," Gabriel told the import–export mogul.
Although Milton couldn't possibly know, the Spanish cut-
lass, the Civil War saber, the Arab *jambiya*, and the Kukri
fighting knife were, indeed, "souvenirs" Gabriel had
stripped off "targets now on ice." Booty taken from assassins
he had gone up against in personal confrontations. Assassins
who had come to wish they had chosen another profession.

"Get to the point, Milton. I've got a boat to take care
of."

Milton's expression turned grim as he sat down on a
small black leather couch. "The point, yes." Milton laid the
briefcase down on the floor, opened it. From the briefcase
he took a photograph and a tape recorder. He handed the
photograph to Gabriel. "My daughter, Pamela. I'm sure
you've heard of *Sadi*, the latest scourge in international
terrorism?"

Gabriel studied the color photo. A beauty with long
black hair and blue eyes, Pamela Milton was standing next
to a swarthy, dark-haired man with a beard and mustache.
She was smiling. The man, an Arab, Gabriel assumed, was
grim-faced, his eyes cold, lifeless except for that subtle
stamp of death worn by one who had time and again seen
death.

"Yeah," Gabriel answered, "I've heard of the cocksuckers. What do they have to do with your daughter?"

Milton turned on the tape recorder. A second later, a
gravelly voice that sounded as if it came from the bottom of
a tomb filled the cabin.

> . . . *I am Muhmad Hammadi, leader of the
> Sword of Islam. I have kidnapped your daughter,
> Pamela, from her campus at the American Uni-
> versity in Washington, D.C. As leader and instru-
> ment of Muhammad, as a true disciple of Allah in*

11

*our* jihad *against the infidels and oppressors of all Islamic peoples, I am demanding a five-million-dollar ransom. You will deliver the money to a contact I will arrange for you to meet in Tunis in two weeks from delivery of this message. If you do not, your whore will die . . . horribly . . . in pain. Every day you do not meet my demands, I will mail a piece of your whore to your home in San Francisco. Do not fail to meet my demands. I will not fail in handing out a just punishment if you do not follow through . . .* Bismillah irrahmam irrahim—*the slut will die* . . . Allah akbar.

Yeah, Gabriel bitterly thought . . . *In the name of Allah, the compassionate and merciful, the slut will die . . . God is great.* But Islamic terrorists are shit!

Angrily, Milton snapped off the tape recorder. He was trembling, jaw clenched. He cracked a knuckle.

Sensing the violence in Milton primed to explode, Gabriel set the photograph down on the coffee table before the mogul.

"All right, Milton. So what do you want?"

"This. In my line of work, I've had to use the mercenaries before to protect certain overseas investments. I never have liked dealing with their kind. They're ruthless, greedy, cutthroat. In short, I don't trust them. . . ."

"But you've used them before."

"Yes. Because, despite what they are, they've always gotten the job done for me, they've always sanitized a situation. But, you're not just a mercenary . . ."

Gabriel blew smoke in Milton's direction. He felt his heart skip a beat when he saw the dangerous glint in Milton's eyes. Milton just didn't know *something*—he knew a lot.

"I know a lot about you, Mr. Gabriel. You're not just a mercenary, nor any ordinary man."

"The only way you could know what you claim so far to know about me is through . . ."

"Them—right. The Company. All right, I'll admit I have contacts in the CIA, Special Operations Division, specifically. They've been responsible before in hiring out to me what they call 'the animals.' Mercenaries. Paramilitary operatives."

"So, they know I'm here."

"Right."

Damn, Gabriel thought. Teeth gritted, he felt the blood pressure rushing straight into his ears like the crash of waves.

Milton saw the fire in Gabriel's eyes. "Now, hold on a minute, let me explain before you start passing judgments. This isn't a setup, I swear to Christ it isn't. And the Company didn't send me here. All you have to do is read the newspapers to see I'm telling the truth about my daughter."

"Mr. Milton, take a good look at that photo. Have you ever heard of Patty Hearst?"

Rage flared into Milton's eyes. "If you're implying my daughter's willingly run off with this pack of murdering—"

"Think about it. She's standing there, grinning from ear to ear in that picture. My guess is maybe she's just run off for a couple of weeks for a good time with her Arab boyfriend, Muhmad the happy dungeater."

Milton thrust a violently shaking finger at Gabriel. "You listen to me . . . that's impossible! I hate these fucking Muslim camel-humpers, and my daughter knows it. She'd never go against me in something like this. I have money. I have power. I'm a prime target for terrorists to extort. My daughter has been set up, used, I'll bet my life on it."

"You already have."

"Listen, even if she is with them in this, she knows she'd never get a dime in inheritance. If—I repeat, *if* that's the game she's playing, then I don't know my daughter at all."

"Maybe she can't wait that long for Daddy to check out."

"God damn you! I came here to offer you one hundred thousand dollars to get her back and kill these bastards and you stand there and insult me."

Gabriel was unaffected by Milton's fury. He stood there, as cool as an autumn breeze in Vermont. At one time Milton had been in bed with the CIA. Strike one. Milton could still be involved with the CIA, and the Company just might have sent him to Key Largo for their own personal business. Strike two. One more strike and Gabriel was going to start backhanding people. Then he thought about that hundred thousand dollars Milton mentioned. No, he didn't really need the money, but having a few extra dollars never hurt. Besides, there were two reasons why Gabriel began giving Milton's offer serious consideration. One—he wanted to get back out there in the killing fields and take the fire to bastards like *Sadi*. Two—five other Americans had been kidnapped in Europe by Sadi. So there were other lives at stake besides Pamela Milton's. The mogul had neglected to mention that fact.

"Before I say yes or no, Milton," Gabriel finally said, crushing his cigarette out in a silver ashtray, "I've got to know exactly what you know about me. Everything. *A* to *Z*. And you'd better come clean and straight."

"Very well . . . from *A* to *Z*." Milton cleared his throat, pulled a silver cigarette case from out of his jacket pocket. With a silver Ronson lighter, he fired up a filtered Camel. Looking Gabriel dead in the eye, he began. "Should I start with your father or your brother?"

Gabriel felt his guts knot up with rage and hurt. "Neither."

Milton drew on his Camel, let the smoke filter out his nose. "I thought you wanted it from *A* to *Z*?"

"Go on," Gabriel growled.

Again, Milton cleared his throat. "Your father, Colonel Charles Gabriel, U.S. Army Special Forces, played a significant role in the conception of the Special Forces in 1952. Quite a man, your father. Two Purple Hearts, a Congressional Medal of Honor. Both of you were cited by President Johnson . . ."

"Anybody can get their hands on that information, Milton."

"But not about the role you and your father played in this country's longest and costliest war. That's classified. That's ultrasecret."

"That's CIA."

"That's right. That's the real picture, Mr. Gabriel. And what I know is *the* reason why I chose you to be the man for this mission—for this, shall we call it, contract for slaughter."

His father, Colonel Charles Gabriel. Suddenly, Vic Gabriel found himself lost in bitter thought, painful memories that had lingered for years. He heard, but he really wasn't listening to Milton.

"After the Korean conflict," Milton went on, "your father raised you and your brother, Jim, at an isolated ranch deep in the Colorado Rockies. Your mother, Patricia, was a nurse in a MASH unit. Her base was shelled and she was shredded beyond recognition."

Gabriel felt his fist clench. *The sonofabitch doesn't mince words. Right to the fuckin' ugly truth.* Gabriel moved to the far corner of the cabin. There, he fired up another Marlboro with a flick of his Zippo. Gabriel hurt, deep inside. As much as he didn't want to hear what Milton had to say, he had to know what the man knew. For his own safety, and for some peace of mind if he accepted this "contract for slaughter." So far, Milton was dead-on accurate in his intelligence gathering. But there was more . . . much, much more.

"Your father apparently had plans for you and your brother."

15

There was no *apparently* about it, Gabriel recalled. Even as he stood there, marooned in the living hell of a nightmarish past, Gabriel, for better or for worse, owed his father for developing, nurturing, honing his lethal martial skills. But his father, who had been a deeply religious and spiritual man, helped young Vic shape a philosophy of life, a way of living, yeah, that let a man walk with his head up, able to look anybody straight in the eye. A simple, direct philosophy. A philosophy of honor and pride. Some might say too simple a philosophy. Maybe simply a tough-guy philosophy. Let them think as they liked, Vic Gabriel had carried his father's spirit, worn that philosophy in his heart throughout the years. Glancing at Milton, he remembered a small portion of what his father had said to him as a young warrior.

"As part of the Seventh SFG, you and your father led several successful penetrations into Laos and Cambodia." Gabriel heard Milton ramble on in the outer limits of his attention.

> . . . *be your own man, your own person. Hell, if someone doesn't like it, that's their tough shit. Listen, son, there's right and there's wrong in life, good and bad in every man. The gray areas are created by people who don't, won't, or can't choose between right and wrong. Do what's right, Vic, not just for yourself, but for the good of others. If you do, you will always walk straight and tall, with your head held high. Every man makes mistakes, sure, but learn from them and get it right the next time, or you might not get a third chance. Life, son, is a trial by fire, especially for the warrior. Follow the good in your heart and you won't every have to compromise. With any man. In any situation.*

Strong words, Vic Gabriel knew, from a strong man.

*. . . remember the voice inside, son. Your conscience. The voice will guide you . . .*

". . . after racking up one of the best NVA body counts, SF started seeing you and your father as a Special Project. This Special Project made at least eighteen known behind-the-lines penetrations that resulted in the terminations of top NVA brass. Nine successful E and Es, recovery operations where downed airmen were rescued and exfiltrated from enemy rear areas. Three breakouts of American and Montagnard POWs from NVA prison hells. After Operation Mudslide, during which the Seventh SFG wiped out the notorious tunnel rats in Chu Lai and Danang, a Company operative by the name of Michael Saunders came snooping around . . ."

"Saunders," Gabriel cut in, jerked back to the present by the mention of the man responsible for his father's death. There was murderous rage in Gabriel's eyes, a sudden blinding fire like the explosion of a supernova.

"I know all about Saunders."

"Then you know the bastard's still alive. And that I'm still looking for the murderer of my father. All right, Milton, you've proved your point. You got this from the CIA."

"You knew that already. It was the only place it could come from. We're not dancing around any secrets here."

"So, let's move on with it. I don't need to hear any more."

"Fine," Milton said, and stubbed his cigarette out in the ashtray. "Does that mean you accept my offer?"

Gabriel blew smoke. "I accept—but on certain conditions."

"I can't promise you that I'll agree."

"Then you're fucked, and you're gone."

Milton squared his shoulders, anger in his eyes.

"I don't really need you, Milton, but you need me. For

weeks now I've been watching this *Sadi* walk all over Europe and nobody, particularly not Uncle Sam, seems capable of stopping these bastards, of giving them a taste of their own poison. Now listen good, Milton. Your deal stinks. You stink. But I'll take your money and your offer. These are my terms.

"This isn't a mission for a solo gun. I go, but I choose my own men, my own MO."

Milton shrugged. "Fine. Then I provide all transportation and armament."

"Fine with me. I want cash up front."

"Half now . . . half on completion."

Gabriel was rolling. He had Milton right where he wanted him. "I've got three men in mind. It will take maybe a week to find and round them up. I can't even guarantee they'll even accept your contract."

"Would fifty thousand per man help influence their decision?"

"Probably," Gabriel admitted.

"I can't wait a week," Milton said, shaking his head. "Five days, and that's pushing it."

"I'll see what I can do."

"You'd better *can do*. No crap. No delays. No more haggling for more money. When you've, uh, finally rounded these men up, I want to meet them, face to face. There'll be a designated rendezvous site in Tunisia. There, I'll give you the ransom money. But, I want you to be quick about this rounding up, Mr. Gabriel. I want to set this thing in gear quick, understand?"

"You're not the only one."

Milton's gaze narrowed. "What do you mean by that?"

"I mean that I've been considering going after *Sadi* on my own. My adrenaline's racing. I get blind pissed off with fury every time I watch the news and more innocent people get swept up in this terrorist tide of murder and insanity. Maybe you were right about timing, after all, Milton."

Milton grunted, then crooked a smile. "Fate has either

blessed or cursed me, Mr. Gabriel. I suppose we'll find out which it is. Now . . . there's something you'll have to agree to."

Gabriel crushed out his cigarette in the ashtray. He looked out the porthole. The goon squad was in place.

"Go on, I'm listening."

"I'm delivering half up front, that's two hundred thousand dollars, as agreed, to be deposited in a Swiss bank account. The other half of the money will be delivered to you and these men you choose when you bring back the head of Muhmad Hammadi."

A graveyard smile cracked Gabriel's lips. "Bring you back the head of Muhmad, huh? That was an old trademark of mine when I was with the Company. A lopped head in a burlap sack."

"Right."

"In that case, I want an extra twenty-five thousand per man as a bonus. The price just went up. Added risk, you understand."

Scowling, Milton said, "You're pushing your luck, friend."

"I don't care. You pushed and I'm pushing back. Listen, Milton, I'll do this thing with or without you."

Milton heaved a sigh. "All right. You're a hard man, Mr. Gabriel."

"The hardest."

"You know, this contract might just give you the chance to scrub the toilet bowl of the Arab terrorist world clean. It needs sanitizing."

"That would take a lot of sanitizing. But this is a start."

"Right. Hell, if I like your work, maybe there's strong possibility we can do business again."

"I doubt it, Milton. If this thing works out the way I think it can, me and my men will be picking and choosing who we work for, where we go and what toilet bowls we sanitize. There's something else, too, Milton."

"What?"

"There's five other Americans who have been kidnapped by *Sadi*. They'll be coming home, too."

"Look here, I'm not paying for you to get them out."

"No, you're not. If I'm going in for the Stars and the Stripes, it's going to be all the way. Every one will come home. Period."

Milton sighed. "All right. But my daughter better come home in one piece. You show up without her, every dime will be returned. Personally, I don't see now how four men can take on a small, determined army of Arab fanatics."

"You getting cold feet suddenly?"

"No, but . . ."

"But, nothing, Milton. Just stand by and hold your breath and watch."

Milton's eyes glinted with laughter, as he glanced to his side at a book about the Eastern Front. "Didn't Hitler say the same thing about Operation Barbarossa? Something to the effect that the whole world will watch and hold its breath?"

Gabriel wasn't amused. The hell with it, he told himself. For a fleeting second, he wondered just how his father would have approached this mission. Like the whispering of a ghost in his ear, he heard the words of Colonel Charles Gabriel, U.S. Army Special Forces.

. . . *in a world of compromise, good men cannot, must not ever compromise* . . .

# Chapter 3

The white-haired, granite-faced man was just about ready to tear his client's head off at the shoulders with a right roundhouse. The ex-merc-turned-gumshoe had found Dave Gildens's wife, all right. Naked, Lila Gildens had been stretched out in the sack at a flea-bitten roadside motel, her legs hiked up halfway to the ceiling and three young studs driving something home to her that wasn't love. At the moment, Gildens was having a hard time digesting this information. At the moment, Gildens was looking to kick somebody's ass.

"Look, pal," the white-haired P.I. began, "I'm not going to bullshit you, 'cause Zac Dillinger's never been one to dance around with nobody." He stood, unfolding to his full six-foot-three-inch height. He was dressed in a gray sport shirt, black slacks, and black wingtips. He wasn't a sharp dresser, because he liked to spend his money on the finer things in life. Booze, cigarettes, wild women, and peep shows. Clothes were a surface distraction and, no, they didn't make the man. Shaking a Camel unfiltered out of a rumpled pack, the P.I. flicked a brass Zippo, torched the smoke, took a deep drag, and walked out from behind his metal desk. He worked over a strip joint on Sunshine Boulevard. He loved Fort Lauderdale because he considered the town "the pussy capital of the East Coast." The walls and the floor of his office were supposedly soundproofed. Still, he could hear the faint rumblings of rock music grinding its way upstairs. Christ, all he really wanted to do right then was collect from this bozo who couldn't keep his wife satisfied in bed and head downstairs for a chat with Bambi and hopefully achieve some satisfaction of his own. Or was it Barbi? It didn't matter. After a while, women all looked the same to him. Damn, maybe he was getting old—tired, too. But he'd been old and tired at twenty, so what was the difference in another twenty years? He'd seen too much, lived through too much, and, yeah, he was fed up.

"Careful what you say, mister. I'm one smart word away from ripping you a new asshole, you hear me?"

"I hear ya. Like one of the three monkeys, I hear ya."

"And what's that supposed to mean?"

"You figure it out, you're the uptown yuppie boy."

"You're pushing your luck, wiseguy. Pushing hard. You know who you're talking to?"

"Yeah. A punk."

The white-haired man stood in front of an oil painting of Duke Wayne. The rest of the wall was lined with pictures of the white-haired man posing with ex–pro football players and a couple of movie stars. There was a file cabinet in the far corner of the room with a coffee pot on top. Beside the file cabinet was a coat rack. Wrapped around that coat rack was a black leather shoulder holster that held two pearl-handled Colt .45s. He had always been a big General Patton fan. He also considered himself something of a World War II buff and often fantasized that he had his own tank division, driving the Nazis all the way back to Berlin.

"I oughta kick your ass, old man."

The white-haired man grunted. He took a hard look at twenty-nine-year-old Dave Gildens. Gildens was big, six-foot, two hundred pounds of solid muscle. He ran an ad agency out of Miami, so he had some money. Unfortunately for the ad man and probably unfortunately for his agency, too, Gildens had his money tied up in nose candy. Worse— the P.I. had done some digging of his own on Dave Gildens:

the guy was a freebaser, dropping ten to twenty grand every couple of weeks on the deadly snow to cook it into rocks the size of Gibraltar. Gildens was high at the moment: the pupils filled his eyes like two pieces of coal; his movements were jittery, his breathing was hard. No telling what he would do, and the P.I. was prepared for any kind of irrational act. Such as violence.

"Listen, I know you've got a habit, Davey boy," the detective went on. "You've been blowing through snow like a plow in Maine in January."

"That's none of your fuckin' business, old man!"

"Maybe . . . maybe not. But maybe your wife got tired of your habit, you think, Davey? Maybe you've been so high on that shit you couldn't get a hard-on to save your life. Whatever . . . it's like this now, Super-Yuppie. So let me spell it out for ya. Lila-baby's a cheap tramp. A whore. A slut. Hey, look," he said, seeing the storm set in his client's eyes but not giving a damn, "I don't know how else I can tell you the truth. I've got the pictures. I've seen it all through a keyhole and another hole you could drive a truck through. And Davey, I'm not in the business of mending broken hearts. You wanna divorce her," he said, thinking he was really rolling now and feeling good in some twisted way over slapping his client with the ugly truth, simply because he just didn't like the guy, "go ahead, because at this point that'd be the best thing for both of ya. She can spread; you can smoke. Everybody lives happily ever after."

Why he turned his back on Gildens, he wasn't sure. Maybe he was hoping Gildens would charge him from behind. Maybe he just wanted to admire the Duke, the big guy all saddled up and riding out with guns blazing. Whichever, he was unaware for a heartbeat that Gildens was, indeed, racing up on him from behind with fists clenched, a bull gone berserk after the matador that's gored him.

"Look, Davey," he went on, gaze held on the Duke,

"she was spreading her ass for half the stiff dicks in this state and some points beyond Florida, north and west. Try to be a man about it, huh? You owe me nine hundred and fifty, not including expenses. I racked up a pretty hefty bar tab on this one, too. So, let's square up so we can—"

*Crack!*

The first thing he felt was the sledgehammer blow to the side of his head. The second thing he felt was the cold plaster of the wall against his face. Then he heard the ringing in his ears. Finally, the floor rushed up at his face, and he figured he was going down for the count.

Gildens kicked the P.I. in the ribs. "You rotten bastard! I'll kill you! I'll kill you!" Suddenly, a strange laugh ripped from Gildens's throat. "Hell, I thought you were supposed to be so bad? Don't they call you 'Bad Zac'? Bad Zac Dillinger is a sad sack—I'll tell the world!" he howled, and drilled another kick into Dillinger's side. "A sad sack of shit! I'll make it so you won't ever work again in this town, tough guy. I'll make it so you won't even be able to look at your ugly face in the mirror ever again."

Dillinger felt Gildens wrench a handful of his hair. That cleared away some of the cobwebs. Twisting on his knees, Dillinger submarined an uppercut, buried his fist deep in his client's gut. As Gildens belched air, his face twisted in pain and surprise, Dillinger bolted to his feet. Enraged, he thunderclapped a right cross off his client's jaw. Gildens backpedaled across the room. Dillinger took a step toward Gildens, full of fury, looking to break the guy of his cocaine habit forever by snapping his neck like a pretzel.

Gildens jackhammered a foot into Dillinger's stomach. As if he'd been hit by a runaway Greyhound bus, Dillinger crashed into the wall behind him. Paralyzed for a second by the blow, Dillinger slumped to his knees. Bracing himself against the wall, Dillinger clambered to his feet. Then he saw it. And he exploded.

The Duke hung askew, the frame cracked, the glass

shattered, a hole the size of a grapefruit punched in the middle of the painting. *God . . . damn it! Nobody fucks with the Duke.*

Gildens was right on top of Dillinger, fist drawn back to deliver a face-breaking blow. A straight right from Dillinger, though, thrown with the speed of a wink of lightning, and Gildens found his mouth filling with blood from a nose that burst like a fire hydrant torn out of a sidewalk. Amazingly, the guy recovered from the punishing blow. Normally, Dillinger had seen a punch like that fell a victim as if a 5.56mm slug from an M16 had cored through his brain. Not so with Gildens. The guy had a heart full of hate, and Bad Zac Dillinger knew he was in for a terrible fight. Dillinger decided Gildens could hold his own weight for a yuppie; the guy had some thunder and lightning in his punches.

Gildens slammed a hook kick off the side of Dillinger's head. With two hundred pounds of brute force behind Gildens's kick, Dillinger flipped over his desk. Grasping the edge of his desk, Dillinger tried to haul himself to his feet but his legs wouldn't move. His ears chimed . . . *I think I'm hearing my death knell.* Fear lodged a ball of ice in Dillinger's guts. Fear, though, he knew, was a tool that could be used. Enough. It was time to finish business with his client.

Through the roar in his ears, Dillinger heard the guy actually laughing, then the P.I. heard Gildens moving toward his desk. Gildens was in for a ball-busting surprise, Dillinger thought. Or hoped.

"Big tough guy. Big Bad Zac. You can bust me up, Bad Zac, I got a checkbook right here in my jacket. Hah-hah. Fuck your nine hundred fifty. Fuck you."

Money, Bad Zac thought. Christ, he could use that bread. Sometimes pride wasn't enough.

Dillinger slid open the bottom drawer of his desk. He reached inside the drawer, felt the cold brass beneath his hand. He slipped his fingers through the rings and launched himself to his feet, in flight and on target like an MX missile.

One roundhouse sweep of Dillinger's right hand, and the brass knuckles whiplashed across Gildens's jaw. There was a sickening crack of bone. Dillinger drew the brass-knuckled hand back again, but he saw the light fade instantly in Gildens's eyes. Gildens wobbled for a split second on rubbery legs. He teetered like a drunk, then dropped, stiff as a board, thudding to the floor on his back. Out there in lala-land.

Zac Dillinger heaved a breath, spat blood out of his mouth. He looked at one shattered Duke Wayne, cursed. He fished a Camel out of his pack on the desk, flicked his Zippo. He took two deep drags, waiting for some of the adrenaline to burn itself out. When he withdrew the cigarette from his mouth, he looked at the bloodied paper. Ah, the bittersweet taste of victory, he thought. Right. Nothing but a mouth full of blood. He checked his teeth, and found a couple of them loose.

A crooked grin froze on Dillinger's lips. He bent over Gildens, checked his client for a pulse, found a heartbeat. A manslaughter rap he didn't need. He was already in danger of losing his license for shooting a rapist on a Miami beach six months back. Luckily, the rapist also turned out to be a notorious drug dealer and the cops had been glad to zip the plastic up over his face.

"Okay, Davey-boy," he said, reaching inside the guy's jacket. "As I recall, you owe me nine hundred fifty bucks. Plus expenses. Plus aggravation. Plus a good bottle of VO. Nah . . . make that two bottles and a case of Pepsi."

Dillinger opened the checkbook. He took a pen off his desk, wrote in thirteen hundred seventy-five dollars as the amount. To be paid to Bad Zac Dillinger. Davey-boy could sign the check when he woke up and found himself staring down a pearl-handled .45.

Moving behind his desk, Dillinger opened the top drawer. Top shelf was what he was after. He opened a bottle of Jack Daniels and poured himself a healthy shot in a coffee cup. He sat down on top of his desk, rubbing his face. He gulped the whiskey, let his head slump on his chest. He was tired and he was hurting. He hated the life he was leading now and wanted out. But what could he do with his life anyway? He had no skills except for head-busting and peeping in windows after cheating spouses. He'd been a mercenary once, but that had been long ago. And anyway, the soldier-for-hire kind of life wasn't any better—in fact, it was worse. So what was left? He couldn't screw for money, because he was too damn ugly, and he didn't exactly like the idea anyway of going to bed with old broads that looked like shriveled prunes.

"And here I was hoping to find you'd cleaned up your act."

Dillinger jerked his head up. In his doorway stood a man dressed in black, from sport shirt to wingtips. Hanging on his lip was a Marlboro he'd just fired up with an engraved, gold-plated Zippo. And a graveyard grin was frozen on those thin, bloodless lips that Dillinger would recognize anywhere.

"Well, I'll be damned—Vic Gabriel. What in the world . . ."

Gabriel stepped into Dillinger's office, closing the door behind him. "I'm almost afraid to ask what happened here," he said, looking pointedly at the brass knucks still wrapped around Dillinger's fist. "I thought I missed the hurricane season."

Dillinger looked at his brass knucks, grinned. "It's called 'client misunderstanding.'"

"Misunderstanding that you're the baddest sonofabitch to ever walk through the valley of death."

"Next to one Vic Gabriel." Dillinger stood, offered Gabriel his hand. They shook. "How the hell you been? What are you doing here? God damn, what's it been, three, four years?"

"At least."

"Yeah, at least. Hey," Dillinger suddenly said, and sorrow touched his blue eyes. "I heard about your father. I'm sorry. He wasn't just one of the best, Vic. By Christ, he was *the* best. It ate my guts when I heard."

Gabriel sucked in a deep breath, a strange smile ghosting his lips. "What do they say, Zac? If you survive your past, you've earned your future?"

"I've heard tell. What can I do for you, V.G.? You wanna go downstairs, drink a few, stuff some garters with tens and twenties? Just like old times."

"I'm afraid the old times have given way to something else, Zac. It's called old age and a heart hardened by the world we live in."

"Tell this old warhorse about it, huh, V.G."

Gabriel drew deep on his smoke. "V.G.," he thought, sounded a little too much like *VC*, but Dillinger had always called him that affectionately. "How's the business, Zac?"

Dillinger looked at Gabriel for a long moment. "Shitty. Just like our days in the bush down in Central America. Bullets and buzzards with few good broads in between. Chasing down some squirrel who owes you more than chump change. I'm the most wanted man around, and it's not because some chick wants to plant her lips on this pretty mug, either. I'll tell ya what, being a P.I. isn't all it seems on TV. Anyway, those guys are a lot prettier than I am in my wildest wet one. Hell, how bad you really want to know, Vic?" Dillinger grunted. He sensed that Gabriel wasn't just asking to hear himself talk. His old drinking and whoring buddy from the Central American days was there for a reason. A grim reason, he suspected. Was the CIA hot on Gabriel's trail again? If they were, then Dillinger suspected he was on somebody's "terminate with extreme prejudice" hit list, too.

"Just tell me. Point blank."

"All right, it's like this. I'm fed up, Vic. At the end of my goddamn rope. It's twisting me in the wind and the noose is cutting right through my skin. This life isn't for an old warhorse like me. I'm living in a sewer, wading through the puke other people make of their lives. I'm sick and tired of being sick and tired. I got debts I can't pay off in a million years unless some relative I've never heard of drops dead and leaves me a bundle, and even then I'd be tempted to piss it all away in Vegas. I got cops all up and down the Atlantic seaboard breathing fire up my ass, threatening me at least once a day to take my license away. Every dime I do make goes to two ex-wives who got the best damn lawyers in town ringing the phone off the hook. Christ, I never had good taste in women, Vic, and it haunts me to this day. I can see 'em all, laughing at me, in my dreams at night. My balls in one hand, a knife in the other hand. Those two bitches and their shysters are raping me bad, those fucking cheap, gold-digging sluts. Hell, what more you want? You know my past. You know I took a commie slug a little too close to the heart down there, and maybe that made me lose a little heart."

"I don't think so. Heart's something you've always had, Zac. Plenty of heart. It's your heart I've got in mind, bad one. You wanna come back?"

Dillinger looked at Gabriel, confused. "As what? A merc?"

"Not just a merc. And not just on any principal's payroll either. Let me give you the story. And I need a yes or a no right now."

"Okay, shoot, V.G. I got all the time in the world . . . that is, before Bambi hits the stage downstairs anyway."

And Gabriel shot from the hip, straight and true. He told Dillinger about his encounter and conversation with Bradley Milton. Intently, Dillinger listened. Gabriel covered everything, the whole grim exchange. By the time the former CIA assassin was finished, Zac Dillinger had fired up his third Camel unfiltered.

His butt planted on his desk, one leg dangling, Dillinger looked at Gabriel for several stretched seconds.

Finally, Bad Zac let out a whistle. "Man alive." He shook his head. "I've been looking to hold the wrong edge of the blade again, but I wouldn't trust this Milton character for nothin'. I can already feel the wrong edge slicing over my palms. Right to the bone."

"I didn't say I trusted him. I've got half of my cut stashed. I brought your half with me."

Dillinger's eyes lit up. "Tax free?"

"What do you think?"

"Stupid question, just thought I'd ask for my own peace of mind."

"You tackle this one, peace of mind is the last thing you'll get."

There was no decision for Zac Dillinger to make. A lot of money was up for grabs. Money that could clear him with a lot of people, set him up in style. Besides, he needed that edge again. Needed it bad. Forget the risks, forget whatever headaches might be involved: Vic Gabriel was the one, probably the only man in the world he'd ever known who would play it straight with his own kind—the warrior.

"Who else you got in mind for this one?" Dillinger wanted to know.

"An ex-Recces commando raising sheep in the Transvaal. I did some digging yesterday through an old contact of mine in the soldiering business and he gave me the lead. You don't know him, but we can be there, I hope, within two days. The other soldier you know pretty good. Johnny Simms."

Dillinger cocked a smile at Gabriel. "Johnny-Boy," he laughed.

"You know where we can find him?"

"Hell, last I heard that crazy little black sonofabitch was in Virginia Beach, hustling pool or street fighting for a buck, something along those lines. But it's all strictly hearsay now."

"Does the hearsay say he's still there?"

"I can check."

"Let's get on it then. Time's wasting."

"Johnny Simms." Dillinger chuckled. "This oughta be some reunion. The three of us did hard time down there."

"We did hard time, all right. But Johnny-Boy owes us. Let's see if he remembers that tab."

Dillinger was shaking his head when Gildens groaned, stirred. Standing, the white-haired P.I. walked to the coat rack. "'Scuse me a sec here, Vic."

Moments later, Gildens, rubbing his jaw, tried to sit up. Dillinger speared his knee into Gildens's back. Gildens cried out in pain, cursed. With hate-filled eyes, he looked up, found Dillinger grinning, the P.I. aiming one of his pearl-handled Colt .45s at his face.

Dillinger laid the check down in front of Gildens, handed him a pen. "Sign."

Gildens signed the check.

"Will ya pour me another shot of JD, Vic? Damn, but I'm feeling good about life again!"


They were like two ghouls, wrapped up in their talk about torture and punishment, and Bradley Milton III wondered if he could stomach their conversation much longer. Taking a sip of his beer, he turned his attention toward the stage for a second. There, a long-legged blonde who had nothing on but a black garter and pink pumps gyrated to blaring rock music. She had hair like sunshine and the roundest, most beautiful ass Milton had ever seen. The strip joint was packed with local Miami riff-raff, drunken men laughing with eyes full of lust while other patrons stood before the blonde Valkyrie and stuffed her garter with money. Disgusted with himself for getting talked into the eleventh-hour meeting at a haven for derelicts and perverts, Milton sat in a far corner booth with the two CIA operatives, code-named Sprenger and Torquemada.

Troubled over the predicament he found himself in,

Bradley Milton worried about his daughter. Perhaps she *was* in bed with this Muhmad Hammadi creep. That thought had never crossed his mind until Gabriel had mentioned the possibility. By God, if she was . . . Milton didn't even want to think of what he would to do to Pamela if she was sleeping with the leader of the Sword of Islam. He knew that he would do more than just strip her of her inheritance.

Whatever the future held, though, the mission was out of his hands. All he could do was stand outside what was certain to become a ring of hellfire. All he could do was wait. Someone would win; someone would lose. Life and death: there would be no in-betweens, no gray on this one. Just black and white, with a splattering of red—blood. The blood of *Sadi* or of Vic Gabriel and his hand-picked mercs. Gabriel was good, all right. But was anyone good enough?

Suddenly, Milton doubted Gabriel was capable of pulling off this contract. Milton liked to be at center stage—always. And he wanted a bigger part now, when destiny was being shaped. He hated being an outsider, an ear listening for news. He hated knowing he wouldn't be there to see Gabriel finish the job.

He was just jumpy. Gabriel would pull it off. He'd bring back the head of Hammadi. He'd better—or Milton was going to enjoy minusing one ex-Company hitter about forty thousand in cold cash.

"What did friend Nietzsche say about morality?"

Milton looked at Sprenger. He was a big man with a crewcut and a bullet-shaped head. Sprenger had gray eyes that could look right through a man. Torquemada was slight, with closely cropped black hair, a small, sharp nose, no chin, and pale blue eyes. Torquemada, Milton thought, hardly looked like a killer; in fact, he appeared more like a clerk in a department store. But Milton had it in writing from SOD. Sprenger and Torquemada were straight from "Animal Central." They were they most vicious killers the CIA had on loan. Part of a contract force: SOD borrowed mercenaries, ex-military men, or the best the navy SEALs, air force SOFs, or army Special Forces had in order to fill up a ship of roving death that few citizens in the U.S. knew about. "Wet work" was almost always done by the renegades hired through Special Operations Division. There were a lot of things about the CIA that never made the newspapers. A contract for slaughter was almost a commonplace ritual within the Company.

Sprenger and Torquemada were deadly, and Milton wondered just where SOD had dredged them up. *Probably out of the grave*, he thought. *Maybe straight out of the Inquisition*. He wanted to laugh at his own bad joke. The Spanish Inquisition was something both of the SOD ghouls had covered during the past two minutes. Both ops had the figures of the dead and tortured during that time memorized. According to Torquemada, the actual Frey Thomás de Torquemada had burned 10,220 victims, tortured another 97,321 souls. In Salem more than 200,000 people were put to death for witchcraft during the sixteenth and seventeenth centuries, Milton had learned from Sprenger. Nero and the original "Circus" had also been discussed. Milton had also had a bellyfull of Sprenger's talk of "the blood flowing in the River Tiber."

Both Sprenger and Torquemada had been ignoring Milton since he'd sat down at their table less than five minutes ago. He might as well have been invisible. Impatient, Milton looked at his watch. Check that. Seven minutes, going on eight. He was getting annoyed, feeling himself slowly driven to the edge of rage. He had heard them agree that Will of God governed even the animal kingdom. They had quoted from the Code of Hammurabi. The laws of the Old Testament—*lex talionis:* an eye for an eye and a tooth for a tooth. And then they took it one sick step further. Sprenger and Torquemada concluded that God was a sadist: after all, He had created the human race and given it a world of suffering and death. God was laughing, watching men inflict misery and agony on each other. Did God have any favorites among us? Sprenger and Torquemada debated the question. Hah-hah, they concluded. Did God need any of us? He needed zero of us, they concluded.

Not only did he feel as if he was holding hands with the devil, sitting with Sprenger and Torquemada, but Milton was trapped in a very precarious, indeed treacherous position between the CIA and Gabriel. And his seat might get a lot hotter if Gabriel ever found out.

"Our friend Nietzsche said, 'Morality is nothing more than an expression of expedience,'" Torquemada answered. "Simply put—if murder is permitted by society, soon that society ceases to exist."

"And just what's your point?" Milton wanted to know. "You kill, I'm sure, or you wouldn't be here. Gabriel's killed, I know, and he's going to kill again. So according to Nietzsche, society then should not allow any of you to survive."

"Wrong. Nietzsche's dead," Sprenger said, his lips slitted with a thin smile. "God's dead, but the devil lives. So does the Company. Rejoice, rejoice."

*What a weird fuck*, Milton thought.

"The point *is* Vic Gabriel," Sprenger went on. "Our point is that punishment is the only effective means when dealing with antisocial behavior. You see, there is order even among animals. Man, it would seem, is the only species of animal that can have a willing and total reckless disregard for order and even a contempt for the lives of its own kind. SOD, on the other hand, has its own very special pecking order in the order of its animal kingdom. A unique order. An order where one understands and readily accepts responsibility for one's actions. Both in victory . . . and in failure. There is no reckless disregard for human life among us. Only disregard, period. We know the world will keep spinning on its axis with or without us. We don't care, really, one way or another. That's what separates us from you and them. We've already accepted our deaths. You haven't. Take your daughter, for instance. What makes you think she's even still alive?"

Milton felt raw fury building in his belly. "What makes you think she isn't?"

"Thank you, friend Milton," Sprenger said, smiling. "You just proved my point."

"Listen, all I want to know," Milton said, his voice edged with impatience, "is why you wanted me here. Everything's arranged, and I thought you knew that. I'm a busy man. So let's wrap this up so you can get back to the Spanish Inquisition."

Sprenger smiled coldly. "This *is* an Inquisition. Milton, and we wanted you here in person to hear it from you. We're talking of torture and punishment and death for a very good reason. We just want you to understand where we're coming from."

"Which is where?" Milton growled. "I've done what you asked."

"No," Torquemada corrected. "We've done what you asked the Company, Milton. You may have some clout among certain starched-shirt circles at Langley, but you don't mean spit to us. We led you on to Vic Gabriel. Okay, fine. And you need to know what's ahead. For him—and for you, if you get cute. There is nothing but punishment and torture and death ahead for Vic Gabriel. And the Company will be acting as the Inquisitors."

"You're both weird as hell, you know that?"

Sprenger laughed. "We know. And we love it."

The crowd roared suddenly as the blonde bent over to pick up a ten-dollar bill on the stage.

"Was there any mention of a Michael Saunders by Gabriel?" Torquemada suddenly inquired.

"Yeah. I know this Saunders murdered Gabriel's father or was an indirect instrument in the murder of the father. The mere mention of Saunders's name didn't sit well with Gabriel at all, I could tell that much."

"Colonel Gabriel was neutralized in Paris, Milton, not

murdered," Sprenger corrected. "There's a lot more to the story than you know."

"Not murdered, huh? You couldn't tell that by the fire that stormed up in Gabriel's eyes," Milton said.

"It doesn't matter at this point," Sprenger said, and rubbed his chin thoughtfully for a moment. "The damage was done years ago. Colonel Gabriel knew too much. Vic Gabriel knows even more. His vendetta against Saunders can never reach a decisive blow. The Company wants Saunders, alive and in one piece, for reasons of its own."

"We will neutralize Vic Gabriel eventually," Torquemada said. "We're hoping that maybe he can lead us to Saunders. Maybe not today. Maybe not even soon after this mission. But someday . . . someday . . . all the wild cards will be neutralized."

Milton scowled. "So the company can rest in peace, right?"

"The Company," Torquemada said, "is only at peace in intrigue."

"And in violence and deceit," Sprenger added.

"You neglected punishment," Torquemada said.

"Of course," Sprenger said. "An oversight."

"Weird fucks," Milton muttered.

Sprenger ignored Milton's scorn. "So . . . everything is set, I take it."

"It is."

"We'll be in touch," Sprenger said, as the ops stood.

"I'm sure you will," Milton grumbled to himself, then took a sip of beer.

The crowd roared as the blonde squatted to rake in the ten dollar bill between her legs.

# Chapter 4

The bar was packed wall to wall with the Savage Horde. The bottom rocker on the backs of faded, sleeveless denim jackets declared their chapter as Richmond, their club emblem a wolf with blood-dripping fangs. The bikers weren't Sandinistas, but Johnny Simms suspected these one-percenters were every bit as ugly, vicious, and treacherous as the communist-backed guerrillas he had fought several years ago in the lower Americas. And, no, the Monroe Doctrine hadn't saved his black ass then, and that one-hundred-eighty-some-year-old piece of paper sure wasn't about to pull him out of the fire now. The *Pistolero* Effect was the real, the only governing rule that Animal Man understood, whether it was Central, South, or North America, or Bangkok. No, it really didn't matter to Johnny Simms if the present foe was Sandinista, biker, whoever. Since he'd taken some hard knocks and a couple of slugs in the gut in the Central American bush and been tortured in a guerrilla prison in El Salvador, everyone everywhere he went looked like a Russian assassin, a revolutionary, a commandante, or a so-called Cuban adviser. Or worse: the CIA. Over the years as a soldier-for-hire, Johnny Simms had learned that most of the time it was damn near impossible to tell the good guys from the bad guys. In a bad world gone mad, the only way to survive was to be badder and madder than the next dude. Pull no punches. Go for the throat. Burn a bridge, then build a new one.

"Tough shot, there, little monkey. Like to know how cocky you feelin' now, boy."

Their brutal-sounding laughter rang in the black man's ears. Squatting, Simms checked the shot, eyeballed the angle, squared his chances. It was eight ball time, make or break, win or lose. Nine hundred seventy-five dollars, most of the bills fifties and hundreds, rested on the rail beside Simms. It took a conscious effort for Simms not to look at that Pandora's Box. If he missed the shot, he knew it wouldn't be by much. And Crazy Bill, the beefy, tattooed slug standing beside Simms, would cash in with a bleeder, could probably sneeze on the eight ball and trickle it into the pocket.

*Motherfuck. I must be one crazy or stupid nigger,* Simms thought. *How do I get myself in jams like this? My mouth can't be that big, can it?* Win or lose, gut instinct told Simms he was going to be in for the fight of his life. Five bikers had stepped up to the table during the past hour to try their luck. All had lost. All were good and pissed off. And every one-percenter in that bar wanted a chunk of Johnny Simms. Carved out of his hide with a buck knife. If any of the Savage Horde had a coil of rope on them, Simms suspected he might be swinging from the nearest lamppost, lynched in Virginia Beach, tomorrow's headline, forgotten the day after. General Fortune wasn't anywhere to be found at the moment. Simms was on his own, and the Savage Horde wasn't about to let him walk away with damn near a grand of their money.

He was positioned dead-center on the table, with the eight ball less than an inch off the rail. Tough shot. Sure, Simms had made that bank shot many times before, but with about twenty pairs of anger- and hate-filled eyes boring into him like drills, he was nervous, the adrenaline burning through his veins like molten lead, his heartbeat pounding in his ears. And Johnny Simms was more than a little scared. Then he thought about who and, more importantly, *what* he was up against. "Nigger," and "Little

Monkey" kept buzzsawing through his head, names he hadn't been called since he'd walked the mean streets of Washington, D.C., in his youth. Johnny Simms was determined to make the shot. He was determined at least to slap his hand over their money before all hell broke loose. Pride, Johnny Simms told himself, it was all a question of pride. Hell, with fifty dollars to his name, he had come into the bar, broken ground on their turf, and done it all on his own terms. With grim realization fevering his brain, Johnny Simms was prepared to leave that bar even more broke— busted up, too. As long as he won this game, though, he knew his point would be made. A man alone, with his back pressed to the wall and with nothing to lose and nothing to hold on to but his pride and dignity, can be the most dangerous animal alive.

At five foot eight inches tall and one hundred eighty pounds, Johnny Simms knew he didn't look like much, particularly to a racist, bloodthirsty pack of white trash packing chains, switchblades, and, yeah, maybe even a piece or two or three. But Simms packed some concealed weapons of his own. A fifth-degree blackbelt, his hands and feet were unregistered lethal weapons. He might go down in a pool of his own blood, but somebody was going to pay the price. A hard price. What did they say? he thought. *It's not the size of the dog in the fight . . . but the size of the fight in the dog. . . .*

Smiling through teeth yellowed rotten by tobacco and whiskey, Crazy Bill stooped. A ball of sweat dropped off the biker's beard as he leaned close to Johnny Simms. "Good luck, boy. You and me both know there ain't gonna be no draw here. Win or lose. All of it. Head to head. Know what I mean?"

"Gotcha, Vern."

Simms chalked his cue. He held the biker's mean-eyed gaze for a second. "Thanks anyway, bro, for the good luck wishes," he grunted, then bent over the table, stick in hand.

"One more thing," Crazy Bill said, the smile vanishing from his lips. "I ain't your bro, Little Monkey."

"Right. Forgot. Lost my head, man."

"And you're gonna need more than just luck—hit or miss."

Simms heard someone in the crowd laugh that if he made the shot his head was exactly what he would lose.

Heavy silence filled the bar.

Grim, Simms lined up the shot. "Back at me, Banker." With the tip of his stick, he tapped the left pocket. "Just so there's no misunderstandin', that's the pocket." The top of the stick slid through the O Simms made of his thumb and index finger.

One of the Savage Horde yelled, "Boo!"

Simms searched the crowd for the turkey.

Laughter.

"Hey, c'mon," Crazy Bill told his bros, the lopsided grin frozen on his face. "Let's be right about this. Man's tryin' to shoot, for Chrissakes. Be cool."

Again, Simms bent low over the table.

A quarter rattled from somewhere behind Simms. Suddenly, the opening barrage of a heavy metal rock song exploded.

Without hesitation, Simms stroked the cue ball. Like a bolt of lightning, the cue ball streaked over the green felt. A sharp clack, and the cue ball bounced off the eight ball. The eight ball rolled on a true line back at the pocket to Simms's left.

Someone cursed.

Fear narrowed Crazy Bill's stare.

The eight ball dropped into the called pocket as the cue ball rolled and rolled back at Simms, angling to his right. The Savage Horde held their breath. Finally, the cue ball lost momentum, stopped less than an inch from the right end pocket.

Simms smiled at the Savage Horde. "I shave 'em close, huh, bros? Hey, what can I tell ya? Someone's gotta win and someone's gotta lose. That's the way the cue ball rolls."

Simms dropped his hand over the money. Crazy Bill laid his stick over Simms's hand.

"I didn't hear you call that pocket, boy. Did anybody hear that pocket called?" Crazy Bill asked his brothers. "Turn that shit off!" he bellowed.

Fear, rage knotted Simms's guts.

A second later, one of the bikers yanked the plug to the jukebox out of the wall. The record groaned as the light blinked off in the jukebox.

Crazy Bill snapped his stick in half, the cracking of wood lingering in the cold hush. Tossing the splintered shafts of wood on the pool table, Crazy Bill growled, "I wanna be able to hear this nigger's skull break. Loud and clear. 'Cause I didn't hear this nigger call his shot. I think Little Monkey's tryin' to cheat me out of my money. What do you think, Little Monkey?"

Johnny Simms knew the moment had arrived. He heard the chain rattle from behind just as he saw Crazy Bill's fist craning for his face. Adrenaline bursting through his veins, Simms ducked. The chain swished over the black hustler's head. Crazy Bill's fist plowed into the rail, but that was the least of the biker's pain at the moment. As the chain whiplashed into Crazy Bill's mouth, Simms pistoned a sidekick into the gut of his attacker from behind. That biker, a bald one-percenter with only his two front teeth and a jagged white scar across his cheek, belched air and clutched his punished stomach. Viciously, through his two gritted teeth, the bald one cursed.

Simms snatched up the winner's purse, stuffed the money in his pocket. For a split second, he thought that was a mighty stupid thing to do, considering about twenty enraged bikers were tightening a ring of doom around him, sealing off the front door with a wall of fury.

Spitting teeth out of his mouth, blood soaking into his beard, Crazy Bill cracked a left off the black hustler's jaw. Backpedaling, his ears ringing, survival instinct took over in

Johnny Simms. Do or die. Spinning, Simms pulped a biker's nose to frothy mush with a backhand hammerfist. A switchblade snapped open in the periphery of Simms's vision. The stainless steel blade glinted as it made an arc for the black man's throat. Sidestepping the blade, but feeling the razor-sharp edge nick his earlobe, Simms countered with a reverse spinning kick. The heel of his boot thunderclapped into the side of the knife-wielding biker's face, and Simms could feel the dude's entire faceplate squish, forced sideways by the tremendous blow, an inch out of kilter. As that biker toppled off to the side, down for the count, Simms felt hands claw into his shoulder. Brute barbarian strength thrust Simms to his knees. The black ex-merc knew what was next: they wanted his face plastered into the side of the pool table, a bloody decoration to be mopped up at the end of the night. With that thought in mind, Simms speared the tip of his elbow into the groin of one of his attackers. A howl of agony from above him sent a shiver of pleasure down Simms's spine. But Johnny Simms knew the worst was coming. One pair of grubby hands was replaced instantly by another set of paws. Simms twisted his head, as the bikers batter-rammed him into the side of the pool table. Stars supernovaed before Simms's eyes, and a terrible pain shot down his back. Jerked to his feet by the Savage Horde, Simms was hurled like a sack of potatoes over the table. Facefirst, Simms hit the floor. The first thing Simms did was move his legs. No broken neck or back.

"You're history, Little Monkey! You ain't walkin' outta here alive!"

Simms began to think that maybe Crazy Bill was right. Then he cursed himself for being a defeatist. Instinctively, Simms rolled away from the pack. Simms felt the rush of air as a chain slammed off the floor where his head had just been. Tasting the blood on his lips, Simms jumped to his feet, hammered a straight right into a biker's mouth. Teeth shattered like glass behind Simms's fist. But the strength of numbers crushed in on Johnny Simms. At the last millisecond, he saw the chain coming. He ducked, but the chain caromed off the back of his head. Simms saw the floor rush up at his face, felt the boot plunge deep into his guts. As the wind vomited from his lungs, Simms heard their laughter echo through the roar in his ears.

Then Johnny Simms heard the scream, thought he heard a crack of bone. One, two, then three bikers suddenly crashed to the floor, poleaxed by something . . . or somebody. Who? What?

Simms wobbled to his feet, desperately trying to straighten legs that felt as if they were made of jelly. From here on out, Simms knew there'd be no skill, no strategy in his attack. Just savage instinct. A primordial desire to hurt and maim. The instinct for survival in the face of death.

A biker's face cracked and splattered into a crimson deathmask as that one-percenter rocketed into the side of the bar. Cursing, yelling swirled, a jumbled maze of noise and agony in Simms's brain. He wondered why the fight had all of a sudden moved away from him.

Then Johnny Simms discovered he wasn't as alone in this battle as he'd thought. Help had arrived. Out of nowhere.

Through a haze, Johnny Simms spotted them. Two men dressed in black, from combat boots to windbreakers, surged through the Savage Horde, a cyclone of fists and hook kicks that bowled down anything and everything that stood in their path of mayhem. One of the dudes speared something that looked like a miniature icepick through a one-percenter's eye. Crumpling to his knees, that biker wailed like a banshee, blood streaming down his face. Another biker took a swipe at the second dude's face with a switchblade, only to end up holding a shattered wrist from a snapkick.

"Hello, Johnny-Boy. Where ya been hiding? Long time, no see."

It can't be, Simms told himself, as the two men in

black fought their way through the Savage Horde. Their fists were blurs, as hunters' flesh and bone cracked, splintered, and cut their targeted flesh and bone. No, it can't be, Simms thought . . . Only one man had ever called him "Johnny-Boy" to his face. A friend. A fellow warrior. And the Ninja needle that had blinded and skewered the one-percenter's brain, also known as a *shuriken*, had been one of that dude's choice weapons. Needles, brass knucks, and a pair of pearl-handled Colt .45s. Bad Zac Dillinger.

Wrapping the back of his arm across a biker's throat, cupping his other hand inside the one-percenter's belt, Vic Gabriel dropped to one knee. There was a sickening crack of bone as Gabriel slammed his victim over his knee, breaking that biker's back like a twig.

With a knife-edged hand, Zac Dillinger crushed a biker's throat. The guy gurgled on his own blood and saliva, his eyes bulging as he tried to suck in air. No good. Simms watched as that member of the Savage Horde sucked in nothing but death.

"Nah, nah, nah . . . it can't be! What the hell you two doin' here?" Simms yelled in astonishment as Vic Gabriel and Zac Dillinger linked up beside him. "Don't tell me . . ."

"I'll tell ya. We're savin' your black ass, Johnny-Boy, whaddaya think?" Dillinger growled, then felled another biker with a left cross that splintered jawbone.

"I'll tell ya what, man," Simms rasped, drilling the heel of his boot into the chest of a charging biker. As that one-percenter was catapulted over the pool table, Simms went on, "The cavalry showed up just in time, all right, but I gotta wonder why. Look out!"

Simms bowled into Dillinger as the .357 Magnum bucked in a biker's hand. Glass exploded behind Dillinger as the P.I. tumbled to the floor. Hitting a combat crouch, Vic Gabriel sprayed that biker with a three-round burst from a mini-Uzi that seemed to appear out of thin air. A line of 9mm Parabellum slugs punched open the one-per-center's chest, blood dappling the wall in a greasy crimson-black smear. The corpse slid down the wall, crunched to the floor. The brawl was over.

Simms spotted the special hip holster just below Gabriel's windbreaker, whistled. "Since when did you start packing that kinda heat again, Mr. Vic?"

"Since we got reassigned," Dillinger answered for the former CIA assassin.

"Don't they call that Israeli piece 'Little Lightning,' Mr. Vic?"

"Right."

"Well, thank God for Little Lightning. How'd you dudes find me anyway?"

"Up until now, I was a private investigator, that's how we found you," Dillinger said. "Besides, you owe money to half the people in this town, and I spotted that beaten-up piece of shit you call a Trans-Am from two blocks away."

Simms looked astonished. "A gumshoe. Bad Zac, my man."

Slowly, their eyes burning with hate and vengeance, the Savage Horde packed together around their dead bros. A dozen bodies, some broken and twisted in death, littered the floor around the pool table. Gabriel, Little Lightning trained on the bikers, backed away from the slaughter zone. Both pearl-handled Colt .45s were in Dillinger's hands, the P.I. covering Gabriel's right flank. Sticking close to Gabriel's left flank, Johnny Simms spotted Crazy Bill. The big biker was sprawled on the floor, blood trickling from his mashed nose. With glazed eyes, Crazy Bill stared at the ceiling. Either Gabriel or Dillinger had driven Crazy Bill's nosebone up into his brain. Simms didn't really give a damn right then who had turned out that dude's lights. Crazy Bill's arm twitched once. Dead was dead, and Johnny Simms didn't think too many people would shed a tear over Crazy Bill.

"Game's over, people," Gabriel called out. "Clean up your mess and say goodnight."

"You won't make it far, assholes," one of the bikers warned. As a group, the Savage Horde stepped toward the trio backing out of the bar.

"Zac," Gabriel said as they moved out onto the sidewalk. A crowd had gathered down the street, just beyond the string of Harley-Davidson hogs parked against the curb. "Get our wheels."

Holstering both .45s, Dillinger wheeled, ran down the street.

A siren wailed in the distance.

Simms breathed in the chilly night air, heard the waves breaking against the beach, about two hundred meters away. He looked up at the sky, ignoring the Savage Horde as they massed on the sidewalk. A full moon beamed from a sky twinkling with countless stars. "Y'know, I could almost enjoy this night, Mr. Vic." Simms smiled. "Beautiful out tonight, ain't it? What's better, I'm about a thousand bucks richer."

"Don't get carried away. The night's young, Johnny. And cut with the 'Mr. Vic' crap, all right?"

"Sure thing, Mr. V."

Gabriel looked at Simms, hard-eyed. Simms smiled.

"I know man," Simms said. "Who loves ya?"

A GMC truck stopped behind Gabriel and Simms. Dillinger was at the wheel. The P.I. flung the passenger door open.

"Let's roll, Vic. The cops are comin'."

"The cops ain't gonna stop us from runnin' you down, mister," one of the bikers threatened from the doorway of the bar. "Your ass is grass, and we're the lawnmower."

"Clown's a real poet," Simms muttered. "Where'd he learn to talk so tough?"

"Hop in Johnny," Gabriel told Simms.

Simms didn't need to be told twice. As he climbed into the cab of the truck, Gabriel kicked the first Harley bike over. The hog toppled into the next bike, and, like dominoes, the rest of the Harleys crashed to the ground, metal banging on metal.

Simms laughed. "I always did like Mr. Vic's style," he said.

A second later, as the Savage Horde cursed him, the ex–CIA hitter pulled an MK2 frag grenade from his windbreaker. Holstering Little Lightning, Gabriel pulled the pin, let the spoon drop to the street, and tossed the grenade under the middle bike.

"Shit!" a biker roared, the Savage Horde scattering down the sidewalk.

Gabriel hopped into the truck, slammed the door.

Rubber squealed, as Dillinger peeled away from the choppers.

The frag blast sent twisted metal spinning across the road. Punctured gas tanks erupted, and blinding saffron flashes boiled down the sidewalk.

"Holy . . ." Simms was speechless. He turned around, looked at Gabriel, then Dillinger, and whistled. "I know you dudes didn't come all the way here just to say, 'Hi,' and pull my ass out of the fire. Now, tell me. What are you doin' here?"

"It's about that reassignment, Johnny-Boy," Dillinger said and cracked a grin.

Simms groaned. Bad gut feeling twisted all the way down through his bowels. "No, don't tell me . . ."

"Yeah, Johnny," Gabriel said, as a wall of fire blazed behind the racing truck. "We've got a proposition for you. And I need an answer tonight."

"I remember Central America, man. Bullets, buzzards, and commandantes. Shit, I don't know if I'm up to even listenin' to this one."

"For fifty grand, Johnny, would you hear me out?"

Simms wasn't sure he'd heard Gabriel right. "Say what?"

Dillinger growled, "He said . . ."

"Yeah, yeah," Simms growled back, dark eyes boring into Gabriel. "I heard. All right, for fifty grand I guess I can at least hear you out."

"You're all heart," Gabriel said, a wry twist to his lips.

"That's where the fight is. That's where a man's real strength is."

"That's why we're making this little housecall, Johnny-Boy," Dillinger growled. "We want your heart. So shut up and listen to the man."

Simms laughed. "You're still as sweet-talking as I remember ya, Zac."

"Shuddup," Dillinger growled.

# Chapter 5

"Look, Johnny, let's cut the crap. Yesterday's dead, finished, gone forever. What happened down there doesn't have a damn thing to do with the present. Now if you think it does, well, I think you also know that you can learn more from a bad experience if you look at it from a distance, than you can learn from a good one. Pain lasts, and it can be a good thing because it will get a man off his ass if he's any kind of man at all. The bad times lingers longer for some reason and bad memories can make a man stronger if he doesn't dwell on all the *ifs*. Am I making any sense, Johnny?"

"Plenty. Listen, dead's dead to me, Gabriel, and almost dead is about the worst experience I know. I remember all those almosts, and I don't think I'll ever forget 'em. Besides, the soldier-for-hire business didn't exactly wear well on me. Low pay or no pay, and you're always right there at the edge of your grave. Either that, or you're chasin' down some sonofabitch who owes you ten grand."

Gabriel was getting angry but he kept his temper under control. "Low pay or no pay, the risks are the same for all of us. I don't know what's really eating you, but it sounds like you're making excuses for some reason." It was time to get hard, Gabriel decided, because his timetable was tight enough already. "Look, Simms, either you're in or you're not. If you're not, I've got to find somebody else. Fast. What's it gonna be?"

Simms grunted, looked away from Gabriel. Seated on the bench next to Dillinger, Simms folded his hands in his lap and fell silent.

While he waited with growing impatience for Simms's answer, Vic Gabriel looked out the starboard porthole. As the twin Pratt and Whitney F100–100 afterburning turbofan engines shrieked to maximum Mach 2.5 speed, Gabriel saw the flashing lights on the squad cars below fade to a faint twinkling in the night. They had been chased by the cops out of Virginia Beach, a dozen squad cars, both city and state, hot on their tail for a good eight miles down the interstate. By radio Gabriel had ordered Milton's hand-picked fly boys to be ready for an immediate E and E from the deserted field off the interstate. Destination: South Africa.

At the moment, Simms had brought the operation to a standstill. If he declined Gabriel's offer, a quick parachuting somewhere up I-95 was on the agenda. Gabriel was one word away from handing Johnny Simms a DZ over the highway. Sure, Gabriel could appreciate Simms's one reservation about accepting the deal—losing his neck. But everybody dies, and for the warrior there's only one place to die: on the battlefield in the heat of battle. He was surprised that Simms was so reluctant to join the team. Then again, Gabriel recalled, Simms had sworn he was finished with the soldiering trade after being imprisoned in Central America. One too many close shaves with the devil, Simms had claimed.

The fighter-jet, which Bradley Milton had incorrectly referred to as a Gates Learjet 25C, was quite a warbird, Gabriel thought, purposely distracting himself from Simms. Perhaps Milton was accustomed to jetting around in a Lear, or maybe he didn't know a damn thing about fighter-jets. Whichever, the black-camoued jetfighter, Gabriel knew, was much more than just a Lear jet. As requested, Milton had gotten the dossier on their warbird, code-named Black Lightning, to Gabriel. Similar in shape

to a Lear jet, Black Lightning had the engines and performance capabilities of a McDonnell Douglas F-15 Eagle.
Advanced APG-70 radar and computer-programmable or
manual fire control of two 20mm M61A1 guns, four AIM-7
Sparrow air-to-air missiles, and four AIM-9 Sidewinder
air-to-surface missiles. Top Mach speed was 2,655 kilome-
ter per hour, with a ferry range of over 5,560 kilometers.
With the latest in a sophisticated warning receiver, jammer,
radar homer, and visual augmentation system, Black Lightning was, indeed, one hell of a warbird. If by grim chance
it was shot down in flames, Bradley Milton stood to lose 1.5
billion dollars. Vic Gabriel had to wonder if Black Lightning
wasn't simply on loan from the CIA. If that was the case, he
wouldn't mind demolishing the warbird himself with a
couple of well-placed frag grenades.

Bradley Milton, or the CIA, had also shelled some
money out on the firepower housed in the fuselage of Black
Lightning. Still waiting for Johnny Simms's answer, Gabriel
ran a grim stare over the armament. Neatly piled against
the wall of the fuselage, port and starboard, were four
Ingram M10 subguns, four M16s with attached M203
grenade launchers, one MM1 multiround projectile
launcher, four mini-Uzis, and one XM-174 automatic grenade launcher. There was also one metal bin stuffed with
fragmentation and incendiary grenades, and spare 40mm
grenades for the M203s and the XM-174. Besides sheathed
commando daggers, Gabriel and Dillinger each wore holstered sidearms, the former CIA assassin toting a Detonics
.45 "Combat Master" Mark VI and the white-haired P.I.
carrying his favored Blood and Guts specials. Stuffed inside
the back pocket of Dillinger's light tan fatigues were his
brass knuckles; a pair of Ninja needles were hooked to the
inside of his combat boots.

At the moment, seated on a bench, Dillinger was
eyeballing a Heckler and Koch G-11 caseless assault rifle.
The P.I. whistled as he cradled the West German weapon.
"I tell ya what, our pal, Milton, isn't pulling any punches as

far as firepower goes, Vic. A buddy of mine in the business just got back from Rhodesia or Zimbabwe or whatever the fuck it's called since the Brits tucked tail and ran outta there. Anyway, before I get sidetracked on how much I hate bleeding hearts and the United Nations, my buddy says this thing—" the P.I. had a crooked grin on his lips as held the HK G-11— "can spit out two thousand four-point-seven-millimeter rounds a minute." He patted the casing. "Plastic casing saves the whole thing from shock, some good old manhandling, all the elements. That four-point-seven slug inside of here isn't all that big, but he said he was blowing the tops off commie heads from five hundred meters out."

"You're breaking my heart, Zac, and boring the hell out of me," Gabriel cracked. "But since the G-11 sounds like it'll get your blood running hot, it's yours for the fight . . . If we ever get this show on the road."

Both Gabriel and Dillinger looked pointedly at Simms.

"All right, all right," Simms said. "But I still haven't seen that fifty grand. I wouldn't mind at least gazing for a minute at fifty thousand dollars, even if I don't ever get to spend a dime of it."

"Don't worry about the money, Johnny," Gabriel said, and flicked his Zippo to fire up a Marlboro. "It's tucked away in a safe place."

"Don't worry about the money?" Simms growled, bitter. "Shit, man, that's part of the reason I got the hell out of the business in the first place."

"There have been times we didn't get paid, either, Johnny-Boy, so what's the whinin' about?" Dillinger gruffed.

"You think you were living the high life back in Virginia Beach, Johnny?" Gabriel posed. "Looked to me like if we hadn't come along when we did, you would've gotten stomped into the floor."

"I was holding my own."

"Holding your own what?" Dillinger growled.

"You in or not?" Gabriel wanted to know, and sucked the smoke deep into his lungs.

Simms shook his head, his eyes glazed with dark thought. "Four years in the army. Three tours of Nam. Shot to shit in a hellhole in Central America nobody even really gives a fuck about—unless he's making millions running guns to the contras."

"Yeah, remember that number three, Johnny," Dillinger said. "Three instead of one. You love this shitty life and you know it. I'll admit, two tours is pushin' it, but you must've loved the bush and hated Charlie's guts or you would've done your time and gotten back to the World as fast as you could after tour number one."

"I didn't have nothin' to come back to, man, and nothin' better to do, that was the whole thing. No family. All of 'em split or dead. I had a brother, but it turned out he ended up with a needle in his arm in a fuckin' shooting gallery somewhere on Florida Avenue."

Gabriel looked away from Simms, felt the pain of ugly memories eating down into his guts again. Vic Gabriel had had a brother once, too. Long, long ago. Simms couldn't have known it, but Gabriel had lost his brother Jim to drugs, too. Cocaine overdose, the cops had said. Well, Jim had gotten in debt pretty deep, dealing to support his habit. Vic Gabriel had learned about his brother's death only months after his father's murder. Enraged, alone, with nothing but a heart burning with black vengeance, Vic Gabriel had launched a short but explosive war against the "death pushers" up and down the East Coast. Short—and violently successful. Following that personal battle, to escape the long arm of the law until the heat cooled, Gabriel had tackled his stint as a free-lance soldier down in Central America.

Vic Gabriel remembered his brother Jim as a rebel, undisciplined, bull-headed, vicious, disrespectful, and self-centered to the point of ultimate self-destruction. Colonel Charles Gabriel had trained both his sons to be warriors, both on and off the battlefield. But as it turned out, the only thing Vic's younger brother ever fought was himself. Fought and, yeah, lost.

For long moments, Vic Gabriel thought about his father and brother. Sons. Brothers. Sure, the colonel wanted both of his sons to be warriors, but Vic remembered something his father had said more than once. A warrior wasn't someone who just went to battle to fight and kill the enemy; a warrior went to any lengths to do what was right, to respect others, and to live by a code of honor and decency, even when others around him were not living by such a code. A warrior could well be a man who raised a family, loved his wife, and struggled with the trials of day-to-day living. So where did that leave Jim?

Nowhere. Dead. Jim Gabriel had been a man on a one-way ride down a dead-end street. Hellbound from day one, Jim had gone through life doing nothing for no one, except himself.

But by getting hooked on dope, Jim might as well have stuck a gun in his mouth and pulled the trigger. God! Why had they grown apart? Although he had always sensed the difference in characters between them, Vic suspected there was more to their separate roads than simply a "growing apart."

Was someone born with character? Could it be developed by circumstances or a guiding hand? Or was it the combined result of everything you came into the world with and the lessons you learned the rest of the way? Had Jim been envious of Vic's close relationship with their father? It had eaten Vic Gabriel's guts as he'd searched for the reason his brother had gone down the dark path to self-destruction. He hadn't found that reason. Searching for answers turned to search-and-destroy.

Sure, he'd put a dent in the drug traffic and avenged his brother's death during that bloody, bitter war on the dope-dealing kingpins. But revenge had left Vic with the bitter taste of gall. The blood debt had been honored, but Jim was still dead. And the reasons for Jim's destruction had gone to the grave with him.

"Maybe I've sounded pretty damn wrapped up in myself," Simms suddenly said. "I just remember the bush days down there too good."

"We all remember them," Dillinger growled. "And they weren't too good at all. I took a couple in the gut, too, Johnny-Boy."

"That's just it. You both understand. The lies and the deceit and getting ripped off by so-called sponsors who wipe their asses with ya, then flush you down the toilet. Man, I've hated my life these past years since. The drifting. Always broke. Hustling pool or squaring off with some gorilla in a dark alley for a buck. Thing is, yeah, you both know where I'm comin' from. You been there with me, you seen and know how it is. I couldn't look either of you in the eye now and say no, uh-uh. I can't, and I'm not. If I did, I couldn't ever look at myself in the mirror again." Simms grunted. "Life's a bitch, then you marry one, I guess."

"Then you die. I know. You ever been married?" Dillinger asked.

"No. Knock on wood."

"I'll have to talk to ya about that. I've died and gone to hell twice already."

"Well, you two pulled me outta hell tonight. I owe ya."

"You don't owe anybody but yourself, Johnny," Gabriel said.

"The hell he doesn't," Dillinger rasped, good-naturedly. "Have you forgotten that prison down in El Salvador with the commandante friend?" Dillinger said. "Remember the taco-face with the machine . . ."

"Yeah, yeah, I remember," Simms answered. "He was headin' south with the blade."

"And grinnin' from ear to ear. C'mon, Johnny," Dillinger said. "Where else you gonna go anyway? Where else you gonna have the chance to make a cool hundred thousand without Uncle Sam comin' around with his hand out? And, most important of all, you're gonna be with the only two rotten sonsofbitches in the whole world who can stand the sight of your miserable black hide."

Simms chuckled, but there was a mean look in his eyes. "When you put it like that . . . I guess I got nothin' to lose. Nothin' at all. But lemme ask ya this."

Smoke filtered out of Gabriel's nose. "What's that?"

"This Milton dude. You sure he ain't hustling you?"

"Me and Vic have already covered that."

"But you ain't got it covered, do ya?"

"I told you, don't worry about the money, Johnny," Gabriel said. "I've got half of it squirreled away. We'll worry about the rest when we finish the mission."

"So, where to now?" Simms asked. "You told me you got another merc in mind."

Gabriel hit the intercom button. "Change your course, fly boy."

"I already did," the voice box buzzed. "We're heading out over the Atlantic."

Gabriel turned off the intercom. He didn't know the names of Milton's fly boys, nor did he care to know who they were. But they were supposed to take orders straight from him and not act on their own initiative. Gabriel decided to let the change of course without his approval slide. Next time, he'd speak up. At the moment there were other things on his mind—like rounding up the last member of the team. Like getting on with the contract for slaughter.

"Atlantic?" Simms queried. "Where to now?"

"South Africa. The Transvaal," Gabriel answered, and drew on his cigarette. "We've got one more to add to the team."

"V.G.'s got a buddy there in voodooland," Dillinger explained, as Simms looked from Gabriel to the P.I., "an ex-Recces commando."

"Recces. You mean a South African stormtrooper, don't ya?"

"Something like that," Gabriel answered.

Johnny Simms groaned. "This oughta be interesting."

# Chapter 6

The setting sun was a blood-red eye beyond the gently rolling green hills of the Transvaal. The twilit gloom blanketed the dead and the dying, as long black shadows stretched over the *Veld*. Swarms of flies, as dark as thunderheads, rolled over the carcasses of sheep and cattle, or picked at the blood of a lion twisted in death. The lion's jaw and half of its head had been shot away, and there was a gaping hole in its chest.

Autofire blistered over the sweeping grassland, as the battle raged on in its second day of slaughter. Screams from men in terrible pain ripped through the smoke swirling around the carcasses and the fiery hulls of jeeps and Land Rovers. The *koppies*, small hills that broke up the *Veld*, trapped the whimpering sounds from combatants paralyzed in pain, stretched out in their own blood and leaking guts. Only armed shadows and bloody skeletons of men moved over the kill zone, stalking, hunting with savage determination what appeared to be the only survivor in the ranch house.

Sliding away from a line of bullet-riddled *rondavaals*, a black man in green fatigues, his AK-47 assault rifle held low by his side, closed in on an overturned Land Rover. The flames from the pulverized vehicle licked out at his face, sucking still more sweat from his dirt-clogged pores. The guerrilla wore the face of fear, for the enemy had proven fearless, savage, invincible. Indeed, whoever the enemy was, he was like a ghost-man in that ranch house, able to kill, it seemed, whenever and whoever he wanted. The ranch house, under siege for the past two days by his brothers of the African National Congress, was now less than fifty meters ahead of the lone guerrilla. As he crouched beside the Land Rover, the arrow drilled through his chest, impaling his heart. The arrowhead punched out a hole in his back, a crimson triangle that gushed blood in a slick jetstream. Spastically, the guerrilla toppled to the earth, his trigger finger squeezing off a short burst of the ComBloc lead from the AK-47. The parched earth drank still more blood of the dead. Impotently, 7.62mm slugs chugged skyward.

Satisfied with the fresh kill, the big crewcut man in the sand-colored fatigues moved away from the window in the kitchen. Cautiously, he checked the hallway in both directions. Wheeling around the corner, he headed down the hallway for the living room. The big man stepped over the shattered tusk, which had been shot off an elephant trophy, as he reached the living room archway. His name was Henry van Boolewarke, and he was down to three thirty-round clips for the HK33 West German assault rifle slung around his shoulder. The battle, he figured, was winding down to its death throes. Either his death or the death of the ANC guerrillas—he wasn't sure who would win. But as grimly determined as he'd been since the opening rounds of autofire had been hurled at his ranch, he was going to take another two or three dozen of the terrorist bastards with him before he checked out into the Great Void. Even if that meant creeping up on the bloody murdering *kaffirs*, one at a time, through the flaming rubble of his house and spearing them from behind with his Barnett Panzer cross-bow. Even if that meant incinerating the bastards with Molotov cocktails. The homemade bombs, gasoline Boolewarke had poured into empty wine bottles, were stuffed in a satchel that hung from his shoulder. A firestorm was brewing. He was certain his enemy's next strategy was to torch the house and flush him out—that, or raze the house with rocket firepower. He was surprised they had done neither so far. Perhaps, he bitterly thought, the Russians were too cheap to throw a few RPG-7s at their Marxist bootlickers. Whatever, Boolewarke knew he was in trouble, and death was indeed hungry for his Dutch bones. Forty-five kilometers away from anything that even resembled civilization, he was on his own. And he was down to the last man. Himself. Perhaps, he thought, that was all he needed.

Boolewarke searched the devastated ruins of his *Vesting* Transvaal. Hundreds of bullet holes pocked the mahogany walls. Shattered glass nearly carpeted the floors of every room. Furniture lay splintered among the corpses. And each room, strewn with the bodies of ranch hands who had engaged in mortal hand-to-hand struggles with the enemy, had become an abattoir. Boolewarke shook his head, silently prayed that God delivered their souls in peace to His side. They had been good men, hardworking and honest, and they didn't deserve to die at the hands of murdering savages in a remote corner of the RSA.

Of course, he knew life in Africa was dirt cheap, and living was worse than intolerable for the majority of blacks in the RSA. But he hadn't created the thirty-some-year-old policy of apartheid—literally "apartness." Change—or "evolution" as the black radicals and communists called the turning point in the RSA—or at least a modification of the system, with blacks sharing in the power and wealth, was inevitable, but, Boolewarke feared what would bring that change: anarchy, a bloodbath of a civil war between blacks and whites. A war that would make the Battle of Blood River and the Boer Wars look like minor skirmishes was sitting on the horizon with Four Horsemen. When that day came, Boolewarke pictured Chaka sitting up in his grave and smiling.

An iron wall separated the races, Boolewarke believed—there was no give-and-take between them.

Blacks wanted change to happen overnight. But whites, with more than three hundred years of attachment to the land, since the Dutch East India Company had hit the shores of the Cape of Good Hope in 1652—whites would stubbornly resist a rapid relinquishing of power. Besides the plain fact of racial hostilities, the white minority also lived in fear of an iron curtain. Russia. The specters of Marx and Lenin. Communism pressed upon the RSA, overflowing from a cauldron of violence and treachery. Boolewarke hated communism and communists more than anything in the world. The death of Nazi Germany had only given way to another Hydra that sought world domination. Boolewarke would carry that belief with him to the grave.

Moving down the hallway, crouched and shadowing beneath trophies of elephants, lions, and the rhino he'd hunted and killed in Zaire when it had been the Belgian Congo, the ex-Recces commando sucked in the stench of death and the sickly sweet odor of roasting flesh. The stink of death fanned the flames of fear in Boolewarke's belly, lent his aching muscles renewed strength. He would need all his strength and courage, he knew, for the final onslaught. Death, he determined, would come hard and ugly for him. And, from what he'd seen so far, death, he feared, would not end the atrocity, nor his shame.

As if to cleanse themselves of the shame of falling back in the face of a lone white man, the guerrillas had torched the bodies of the ranch hands and hauled them away from the house. Corpses had been turned into a perimeter of fiery gravemarkers. Even Boolewarke's pet lion, Thor, had been massacred where he'd stood guard at the front gate. During the initial onslaught, two guerrillas with machetes had ripped out the heart of the lion and eaten it in front of Boolewarke's eyes.

There was no escape from the stink of death. Bodies of Boolewarke's ranch hands and their families, both black and white, littered the living room. There, the defenders had made a valiant last-ditch stand with R4 assault rifles against the guerrillas. At least forty bodies of ANC terrorists were sprawled in death, just yards away from the battered living room window. The massacre had been committed less than an hour ago. The shrieks of women and children still pierced the Dutchman's brain, haunting cries that demanded vengeance in blood. During that titanic struggle, Boolewarke had chased down and slaughtered at least ten guerrillas himself as they invaded the house, firing at anything that moved.

Now, the Afrikaaner knew, the guerrillas were regrouping for another attack after licking their wounds. Armageddon was closing down on Boolewarke.

Boolewarke decided his best chance would be to barricade himself in the upstairs bedroom. There were windows on each side of the room, so he would have a clear line of vision all around the compass and an open field of fire on the guerrillas as they amassed and charged. First, Boolewarke checked the discarded R4s. Each man, it appeared, had gone down to his last round. They had fought with such terror and frenzy that several times Boolewarke had to pry a weapon out of a viselike grip. The magazine in each South African assault rifle was empty. All were brave men who had fought the good fight. To lose his life now, he thought, would be to shame their memories.

Unslinging his HK33, Boolewarke rested the assault rifle by his foot. Quickly, bending, Boolewarke cocked the crossbow. Having no foot stirrup, the Dutchman planted the buttplate against his stomach. From his brown leather quiver, he pulled an arrow and loaded the bow.

Glass crunched behind Boolewarke. Whirling, the Dutchman triggered the crossbow. With a drag weight of two hundred-plus pounds, the broadhead hunting arrowpoint missiled across the living room at a velocity of three hundred feet per second.

Autofire blistered the air.

Boolewarke gritted his teeth as the 7.62mm slugs tore across his side. How badly was he hurt? Time seemed to stand still for Boolewarke, and the agonized cry from the living room lingered in his ears. Bullets had sheared away cloth—at a glance Boolewarke checked the wounds. Superficial. Still, the blood flowed, wet and warm, down his side, soaking into his pants. Pain, more pain, was just what he needed to urge him on into the Eye of the Fire.

The shriek, strangled in death, ripped for less than a heartbeat from the guerrilla's mouth. Hand twitching, the guerrilla reached for the arrow speared through his eye.

Boolewarke heard the frenzied movement down the hall. There was no time to load another arrow in the crossbow; the guerrillas had penetrated the house. Knowing a ring of doom was sealed around him, Boolewarke dropped the satchel, then slipped his arm through the crossbow's strap. He might not use the crossbow again, but the all-metal Barnett Panzer bow was inscribed with his father's name. If he went to his grave that day, Boolewarke wanted to know he hadn't let his father down by abandoning the crossbow in the blaze he knew was coming. Unzipping the satchel, the Dutchman hauled out three firebombs. With a Zippo, Boolewarke torched the gas-soaked rag crammed into the wine bottle.

All hell broke loose.

Guerrillas, their AK-47s blazing, hot lead churning up the wall behind Boolewarke, burst through the devastated window opening.

Boolewarke hurled the firebomb. Rolling away from the tracking line of fire, he snatched up his HK33, his other hand fisting the satchel. Teeth gnashed against the fiery waves of pain shooting up his side and sweat burning into his narrowed gaze, Boolewarke triggered the HK33, one-handed, on full-auto. A stream of 5.56mm×45mm slugs stitched an ANC goon across the chest. Howling, the guerrilla spun, crimson drops spraying across his comrade's face.

Boolewarke rolled out of the living room, prepared for anything, prepared even to greet death. As glass dug into his back and side, Boolewarke heard the explosion, felt the floor tremble beneath him. Shrieking lanced the air, and tongues of fire snaked after the Dutchman. Two guerrillas were launched through the window on the crest of the boiling fireball. Three other Marxist rebels were lapped up by the wall of fire, vaulting through the window as their comrades were blown outside. The blast launched those guerrillas outside, right on the flaming slipstream of their comrades. Human torches, those guerrillas writhed on the ground beyond the window, wailing in agony.

The machete craned for Boolewarke's face. Thrusting his HK33 up, the Dutchman blocked the deathblow, metal clanging off the barrel of his assault rifle as he swept the machete away. In the blink of an eye, Boolewarke triggered a three-round burst. The HK33 chattering in his grip, Boolewarke saw the stream of slugs shatter the black face above him into scarlet mush. The corpse toppled onto the Dutchman, autofire drilling into the dead man's chest. More guerrillas tightened the noose. Slugs ripping into the floor beside him, Boolewarke rolled back into the living room. The stench of charred flesh pinched inside his nose with the potency of ammonia, cleared his senses of pain. Fear can be the most powerful motivating force in a man, and Boolewarke reacted to the new threat instantly. Flicking his Zippo, he lit two firebombs, hurled the Molotov cocktails down the hall. He heard the guerrillas cursing, yelling in Bantu. A split-second later they were screaming the universal language of pain, the twin fireballs whooshing down the hallway, sweeping up the enemy in a hellish blaze.

Boolewarke bounded to his feet. What he saw next froze him in his tracks.

A human torch was less than two feet from Boolewarke. Shrieking like a banshee, the black demon raised the machete over his head. Flesh was melting like wax off the guerrilla's face and hands.

Boolewarke snatched up the elephant tusk. With

fear-and-rage-powered might, the Dutchman gored the demon, felt the jagged end of the makeshift spear grate against the guerrilla's spine. The machete clattered to the floor. Still wailing, the human torch backpedaled, charred hands wrapped around the tusk.

Bootsteps pounded down the stairs.

Spinning, HK33 in hand, Boolewarke triggered a long burst. Like bowling pins, five guerrillas toppled down the stairs, bloody chunks of flesh and ragged strips of cloth plastering the mahogany walls. Without hesitation, Boolewarke hurtled another lit firebomb up the stairs.

A roiling cloud of fire engulfed more guerrillas.

Suddenly, a tremendous explosion rocked the living room. A tidal wave of dust, smoke, and rubble washed over the Dutchman. *So Ivan isn't as cheap as I suspected,* Boolewarke thought. So be it. *It's a good day to die.*

Fire raged behind Boolewarke as he ran down the hallway. With a thunderous kick, the Dutchman caved in the door to the garage. Loading another arrow in the crossbow, he moved toward the open doorway. Skirting behind the cover of his Land Rover, he crouched near the opening. Back pressed to the wall of the garage, he lit another firebomb as he spotted the RPG-7 rocket team. The two-man fireteam was kneeling, less than thirty meters from the ranch house. Grim attention focused on the living room, as the human torches burned to shriveled black mummies before them, their screams echoing across the slaughter zone, the fireteam attached 85mm warheads to the RPG-7s. They were either fools for leaving themselves so exposed, Boolewarke thought, or they had balls of iron. Whatever, Boolewarke threw the firebomb with all his strength.

The explosion kicked the guerrillas back, the RPG-7s flying from their hands. Consumed in an oily ball of fire, the guerrillas writhed, screaming as they slapped at the flames eating away their faces.

Running, Boolewarke reached the outer limits of the

ring of fire eating away at his fresh kills. Suddenly, autofire raked the ground beside the Dutchman. In the distance, Boolewarke spotted a group of about twelve guerrillas, their AK-47s stammering.

Scooping up an RPG-7, Boolewarke triggered the warhead. Downrange, the projectile erupted in the heart of the guerrillas. Bodies cartwheeled on tongues of fire. Shredded limbs and bloody stick figures of men rained to the earth. Intently, Boolewarke searched the *koppies* through the drifting veils of smoke. Silence, except for the crackling of angry flames. Were all the guerrillas dead? If they weren't dead, by God, he thought, they would wish they were when he got his hands on them. *They haven't seen savage yet.*

No, not all of the combatants were dead, Boolewarke discovered. A wounded guerrilla crabbed across the ground. Boolewarke spotted the enemy, as he sought cover behind the carcass of Thor.

"Bloody *kaffir*," the Dutchman muttered, his native tongue dripping with venom. "Fucking Soviet bootlickers!"

Unslinging the Barnett Panzer crossbow, Boolewarke cocked the bow, loaded up for the kill. Kneeling, he drew target acquisition, triggered the arrow.

The guerrilla cried out, then lay utterly still, the arrowhead sticking out of his throat.

East, Boolewarke saw a half-dozen guerrillas scattering, running for their lives up the *koppies*.

Henry van Boolewarke was in no mood to allow such a hasty retreat. Standing, dropping the crossbow, he picked up the second discarded RPG-7. The guerrillas had put a distance of a hundred meters between themselves and the Dutchman, who stood behind a wafting curtain of black smoke. With an effective range of 300 meters, Boolewarke knew the Russian rocket launcher was still very much a deadly, useful tool.

The warhead streaked away from the killing field. A

second later, the explosion scythed through the surviving ANC guerrillas.

The RPG-7 fell from Boolewarke's grasp. It was over—or was it? He tasted the gall in his mouth, felt the blood coursing down his side. Fire. Hate. He was alone, with nothing but the stink of death in his nose. Hate, hate, and more hate. Hate was the only thing he could feel at the moment.

And there were no pieces to pick up.

Slowly, he walked toward the carcass of Thor. The hatred he felt toward the ANC guerrillas almost made him puke.

They had shattered his life.

His dreams were dead.

He was grateful he'd never married, never had children to carry on the Boolewarke line: he might have faced a life with memories even more horrible than those he was ready for. Tomorrow. When he awoke and opened his eyes, the nightmare would still be there.

Henry van Boolewarke slumped to his knees. Numb, he touched the carcass of Thor. He shut his eyes, thought about the good men and their families who had perished defending his ranch.

The Dutchman felt the tears burn into the corners of his eyes.

One more battle was over.

*"You live or die by pain. You live or die inside your pain. Physical, emotional or spiritual, if it's not there, you'll pick some up along the way, and you'd better be prepared to deal with it. During the course of his life, a man dies more than once, and by dying I don't mean in the physical sense. Yeah, you die, but you can't stay dead. You pick yourself up, you reborn yourself, sons."*

*Fourteen-year-old Vic Gabriel couldn't quite comprehend what his father, Colonel Charles Gabriel, was saying.*

*As Vic and his twelve-year-old brother, Jim, jogged down the trail that wended through the thick pine and fir forest, he didn't understand what his father was trying to relate to them—not so much in words, no—but he could sense a feeling, a deep feeling in his father's wisdom. Feel it as if he would put his hand near the licking tongues of a campfire. There was always a good reason, young Vic Gabriel knew, when his father spoke in that slightly incomprehensible, almost mysterious way. It was wise to listen to his father. And, if you didn't immediately understand what he said, you would. In time. The old man had been down some tough roads. And Vic Gabriel assumed, with good reason, that his father had died more than once and been reborn. Something inside him told him that his father was trying to warn his sons about life, about the struggles ahead for both of them, hoping that his sons would hear him and think hard about what he said.*

*Pain. Like the pain he was feeling now, as they passed the four-mile mark on their daily five-mile run? The dry throat. The burning chest. The heavy legs, growing more wooden by the mile. The voice inside raging for him to stop and rest. Perhaps, Vic Gabriel reflected, that kind of pain was only part of the rebirth process. But physical pain was only one kind of pain. His father, he sensed, had suffered and endured a more lasting, deeper kind of pain. Those dark, troubled roads, right.*

*Vic looked at his father. Tall. Lean. Chiseled features. Gray around the temples. Eyes that looked you straight and true in your own eyes. Physical appearances, young Vic decided, can tell a lot about someone. Outside, he thought with pride, slowly pulling in the chill Colorado mountain air through his nose, the sunshine warm on the back of his neck, his dad looked every bit the hero he was. Inside, in the heart, lived the real hero. Strong. Tough. Independent. Wise. Caring. Qualities that, even at fourteen years of age, Vic Gabriel could spot. Qualities that he admired and wanted to have.*

"*Can we stop now? My chest hurts, Dad. How come we have to do this every day? Run, run, run. I hate it!*"

There was a tone in his brother's voice that Vic found himself resenting more every day. A whining, pleading voice. The cry of a quitter. Turning, he looked at his younger brother. He found himself almost feeling sorry for Jim. Jim had stopped, was bent over with his hands on his knees. Vic stopped running now, too, as his father turned to look back at Jim. For a moment, Vic thought his father was going to lash out at Jim in anger. But something seemed to soften the hardness in the father's eyes as he stared at Jim. Pity? Jim, Vic knew, hated the morning runs. Hated having to jump out of bed before daybreak and do his chores around the ranch. In fact, Jim seemed to hate anything their father wanted them to do. Why was his brother always complaining? Vic wondered. Maybe the toughness of mind and body just simply wasn't there? Even still, couldn't Jim see that his father was trying to teach them something, trying to make them something better? He wasn't trying to punish them or humiliate them in any way. As the days passed into weeks and the weeks into months, Vic was beginning to grasp more of what his father was saying. Sure, life is pain, and pain is inevitable. Fear is fear. Pain is pain. You have to face it. Face everything that comes your way. Stay centered in yourself, his father would say. Don't be influenced by the world around you, don't let the world dictate you. Dictate to it by staying centered. Just what did that mean? Maybe it meant that in the end, you can only ever rely on yourself and what you've got inside you, Vic believed. Maybe Jim didn't think that way. Maybe Jim didn't see it. Maybe he never would.

"The running, son, isn't just meant to make your body stronger," Colonel Charles Gabriel said in a measured, patient voice. He tapped his chest with his finger. "It's meant to make your heart strong, your spirit tough. Every step toward every mile you're measuring yourself. How far you can go. How much you can take. How much you're *willing to give to yourself and get out of yourself. Are you listening to me?"*

"Dad, I've already heard that life-is-a-marathon garbage before. I'm hungry and I'm thirsty and my chest hurts. I wanna go back."

Now anger did flash into the father's eyes. But, once again, the ice melted away from the look. "All right, another quarter-mile down the trail, and we'll take up a few minutes in what I promised this week."

What was promised was a lesson in firearms. Anxiously, his heart racing with a strange mix of fear and excitement, Vic followed his father another quarter-mile farther down the trail. There, the Colonel stopped a few yards in front of a man-sized dummy. Unzipping his gray sweat jacket, the Colonel removed two M-1911 Colt .45 automatics. He handed one .45 automatic each to his sons. Vic had to hold the .45 in both hands. Having never held a gun before, he was surprised at how heavy it was. He was almost afraid to hold it, fearing that it might go off somehow accidentally.

"That's no toy, sons," his father began. "A gun, like anything else, is a tool. It serves a purpose. Always, always assume a gun is loaded. It . . ."

Suddenly, Vic saw the horror on his father's face. What had happened? What . . .

Whirling, Vic couldn't believe his eyes. For a split-second, he was frozen in shock, his limbs locked up by disbelief and terror. His brother, his own flesh-and-blood brother was standing there, behind him, grinning. And aiming the .45 at him!

Vic felt something inside him snap, felt an icy shiver run down his spine. Some rage, buried deep and dark inside his heart, exploded. Jim started to lower the gun, as if to say he was only playing around. Vic hammered his fist off his brother's jaw, dropped him on his back.

"What the hell do you think you're doing?" Vic heard his father yell at Jim. But the words seemed to come from *a mile away, an echo that bit and swirled through some disbelief that numbed Vic's mind.*

Tears welled up in Jim's eyes. Rubbing his jaw, he stood. "I didn't mean it! I was just fooling around! I wouldn't have pulled the trigger, I swear!"

Father and sons stood in utter silence. Vic could feel the leaden hush weighing down on him. It was incredible that his brother would do such a thing. Sheer stupidity. Or was it? Did his brother resent, dislike him that much? What was that he saw in Jim's eyes? Hatred? Bitterness? Suddenly, the gun felt as if it was twice as heavy in Vic's hand.

"You care about him more than you do me!" Jim screamed, the tears now spilling down his cheeks. "You spend more time with him! You don't yell at him when he does something wrong! I hate you!" he yelled at Vic, then turned and ran off down the trail.

Incredulous, Vic watched as his brother vanished down the trail. Why? he wondered. What was going on inside of Jim? What would possess him to turn a gun on his own brother, even if he didn't mean to pull the trigger? Or did he? It was madness, and Vic had seen the madness in his brother's eyes.

His father's voice still echoed in his head from a mile away.

"I'm afraid for him."

And from that day on, Vic was afraid for his brother, too.

Pain. Fear. Something inside young Vic Gabriel warned him that pain and fear would defeat his brother. Would crush him.

He would die and never rise again. And he would only die once.

It was then that Vic Gabriel noticed there was no clip in either of the guns.

# Chapter 7

They found him with his face buried in his hands. Beside Thor, Henry van Boolewarke sat alone, marooned in a sea of slaughter.

The sun burned down like a furnace over the *Veld*. High noon over hell.

As brakes squealed, Boolewarke's head jerked up. The crossbow in his hands, the Dutchman drew target acquisition on the driver of the Land Rover. Boolewarke's face was twisted with murderous rage.

His gaze narrowed, Vic Gabriel shut off the Land Rover's engine.

Grim-faced, Zac Dillinger unholstered one of his Colt .45s. "What the hell . . ."

"My thought exactly." Gabriel searched the carnage, the wisps of black smoke curling away from the smoldering ruins of the ranch house. Slowly, M16 in hand, Gabriel opened the door, took a tentative step out into the hell zone. Ferocity burned in Boolewarke's blue eyes, the look of a wild, cornered animal about to strike back at its attackers.

"Dutch? Dutch?" Gabriel said, the stench of decay piercing his senses. For a moment, Gabriel couldn't believe his eyes. Death was everywhere. A furious battle had been waged, and Henry van Boolewarke appeared to be the only survivor of the titanic struggle.

Boolewarke didn't answer Gabriel. Instead, the

Dutchman kept the Barnett Panzer crossbow trained on the ex-CIA assassin. Dillinger and Johnny Simms, an M16 in the black man's hands, filed out of the Land Rover's cab, walked behind Gabriel.

"Throw down your bloody weapons or I'll drill you bastards where you stand!"

"Easy, Dutch, it's me, Vic Gabriel."

A bone cracked in Boolewarke's knee as he stood. He looked, long and hard, at the three men, the crossbow shaking in his hands. "Wh-who?"

"Dutch . . . Dutch!"

Boolewarke's lips cracked open. Recognition dawned through the hate in the Dutchman's stare. "Jesus bloody Christ. Vic Gabriel. It is you." The crossbow was lowered and brought to Boolewarke's side. A haunted look settled in the Dutchman's bloodshot eyes. Soot streaked his face. Blood and dirt had caked to black scum on his fatigues. He stood, facing Gabriel, shoulders hunched, limp, as if he would fall over at any second. "Wh-what . . . wh-what in God's name . . ."

"What happened here, Dutch?"

The air rasped out of Boolewarke's mouth. He looked around at the carnage, shook his head. Bitterly, he said, "What do you think? A bunch of savages attacked my ranch, killed all my people, burned my life to the ground, that's what happened. Look around at this . . . look at this! Fucking Marxist spearchuckers," he snarled, then looked pointedly at Johnny Simms. "What's this you brung with you, Gabe? Christ Jesus, just what I need to look at now . . . another stinking *kaffir*."

Simms clenched his jaw. "Hey, man, I'm just along for the ride. I ain't the thorn in your side, stormtrooper."

Boolewarke muttered a curse. Finally, turning his dark stare off Simms, Boolewarke let the crossbow drop from his hands. There was silence for several stretched seconds. Flies buzzed over the carcass of Thor.

"How long ago, Dutch?"

Boolewarke cursed. "I don't know. Two, maybe three days I been sitting here."

Dillinger walked away from the group, the .45 hanging by his side. Incredulous, the P.I. looked at the corpses, kicked at a severed arm. "I guess I don't have to ask who won."

"They did," Boolewarke growled. "That's who won. Might as well have killed me, too."

Dillinger stopped, looked back at Boolewarke. The P.I. was silent.

Gabriel didn't feel it was necessary to press Boolewarke any further about the massacre. South Africa, indeed all of Africa, as he knew from grim experience, from his days as an assassin and soldier-for-hire in Angola, was a mess. What had happened to Boolewarke's ranch was just another headline in tomorrow's newspaper. Racism, nationalism, tribal conflicts, economic rot, and a debt-load that could never be paid off in a hundred centuries—these made Africa a plague unto itself. With no cure in sight.

"Dutch," Gabriel said, realizing he was walking on thin ice that was about to crack wide open, "I need to talk to you. It's about a mission."

Boolewarke grunted. "A mission," he growled, shaking his head, then looking around the slaughter zone. "If it doesn't involve African National Congress Ivan asskissers, I'm not interested."

"Will you hear me out?"

Boolewarke stood in silence for a moment. "*Ja*, I'll hear you out. God knows, I don't have any more to lose than I already have by listening to you. Talk. I'm all ears. Bitter ears. You're looking at a dead man . . . a dead man who needs to come back to life."


Grim-faced, his eyes burning with vengeance, Henry van Boolewarke listened to Vic Gabriel's proposition, all right. Listened and accepted. Under any other circumstances, the Dutchman might not have accepted the contract for slaughter. *But when your world's yanked out from under you and you're face-down in the dirt eating your own guts,* Gabriel thought, *there's nothing left to do but get up and move on.* And if ever a man would be haunted to the edge of his grave by the specter of death, it would be Henry van Boolewarke. He was now in a class, a nightmare, all by himself. At the moment, Boolewarke sat in stone silence. The Dutchman's Barnett Panzer crossbow rested by his commando boots, and a quiver stuffed with arrows sat on the bench beside him. For a reason Gabriel could only guess at, the Dutchman took an Aussie bush hat from the Transvaal hellgrounds. The sand-colored bush hat hung from a chin strap, resting on the back of his neck.

Black Lightning was fifteen thousand feet over the jungle bastions of Zaire. Darkness bathed the far-reaching jungle, but a more fearful darkness was just ahead for the four-man strike force. The darkness of violent death.

The warbird was flying north, en route for the prearranged rendezvous with Bradley Milton III. The team was assembled, and the mission was about to get underway. Gabriel had the fighting force he needed to accomplish the mission. They were all blooded in combat, had proven themselves fearless and savagely skilled, both in a firefight and in the trenches goring it out, hand-to-hand, with the enemy. But Gabriel knew in time he would have to face up to one problem. Bad blood was already boiling between the Dutchman and Johnny Simms. The last thing they needed now was internal conflict over politics. Gabriel suspected he would have to deal with a head-to-head clash eventually. The Dutchman was bitter about his ranch, his life shattered by black terrorists, and Johnny Simms was an easy scapegoat just within reach. It would take a small spark to light the fuse to the human dynamite that was Johnny Simms. Gabriel strongly suspected that the black ex-merc had a definite stance on the subject of apartheid—and even stronger negative feelings about the Boer who was part of the four-man strike force. So far, the Dutchman hadn't said another word about the battle that had left his life in ruins. Boolewarke had appeared numb with shock and grief since the team had pulled away from the killing field in the Transvaal.

Because he had rounded them up for the mission, it went without saying that he was in charge of the strike force. Of course, he wouldn't make a point of his authority or an issue of his command. Respect and trust are earned. And Gabriel had earned them from each man in the Eye of the Fire on battlefields long since flamed out.

Vic Gabriel respected each man for his martial skills and admired them for the time they had done in hell. All right, each warrior had undertaken the mission for his own personal reasons. Some thought it was the money. Some saw it as backing away from the dead-end they had reached in life—or maybe as moving ahead for the light at the end of the tunnel. Some called it patriotism, perhaps. Whatever their reasons, Gabriel had a killer elite in Dillinger, Boolewarke, and Simms. Regardless of past performance, though, they would have to prove themselves again. Just as Gabriel would have to prove himself again. However the mission would take shape, it would be a grim and bloody reunion.

"We did some hard time in Angola, Gabe," Boolewarke said, his voice quiet, as he looked away from the porthole, met Gabriel's stare. "If it weren't for you, my whole squad would've been wiped out in that Cuban ambush."

"It was an accident, Dutch," Gabriel said, and cracked a graveyard smile. "I was only there to put a bullet through that Spetsnaz major general's brains. I was merely exfiltrating when I stumbled across that ambush. Hell, I think I hate communists as much as you do."

"Nonetheless, to this day I've always felt like I owed you."

"That's not why you accepted my deal, is it, Dutch?" Boolewarke's expression turned dark as he looked away from Gabriel. "*Ik heb hem gezien*. I have seen him. He is Death. I've seen him, many times. You've seen him, too, Gabe. We've both been there, more times than we care to remember. Perhaps . . . perhaps I need to see Death again. Death is all I've seen, all I've known. The Great Worm seems to want me bad, worse the older I get. Christ," he said, and his voice turned bitter, "I've been walking with Death, holding hands with the devil since I joined the Recces at nineteen. Seen nothing but a bloody mess not even the Second Coming could straighten out. Africa's gone to hell, and there's no turning back. I look at my roots and all I see is the path to Armageddon in this land when I trace my heritage. The white man's grave, the natives call the Dark Continent." He grunted. "My ancestors fought the Brits, fought Chaka and his Zulus. . . . None of it seemed to matter. Certainly, the presence of the white man hasn't improved much here, except fatten the bank accounts of a lot of Europeans. Christ, both the Boers and the Brits are still sitting on a time bomb and they act like they're blind to it all. Nothing's changed, nothing's gotten any better. In fact, as the days pile up in corpses and skeletons . . . I look at myself, wonder what the hell I can do. A trained parachutist, qualified in both static and free-fall techniques, jumped more than one HALO. The best, my superiors in the Recces said, at seaborne operations. I'm even a qualified paramedic . . . All these skills I've been sitting on for the past few years. Hell, I guess I've just been rotting away. Nothing but a dinosaur in a land about to become extinct."

It sounded to Gabriel as if Boolewarke was speaking just to hear his own voice. Or perhaps the Dutchman was trying to justify accepting the mission against the Sword of Islam. Whichever, Gabriel decided it was best to let Boolewarke air his thoughts.

"What sickens me the most," Boolewarke went on, teeth gritted, "is the naive busybodies who tell us how to run the RSA. Spineless sacks of shit who couldn't even tell you what an Afrikaaner is."

Simms spoke up. "Maybe the naive busybodies just want you to take a hard look at yourselves before this Armageddon arrives. Maybe the way things are isn't that great."

"Maybe you should shut up until you know what you're talking about," Boolewarke rasped. "First of all, if you think for a second American blacks are loved by the African blood, you ought to take a little jaunt through Zululand."

"Listen, stormtrooper," Simms shot back, "I don't particularly like having to do this mission with a bigot who might or might not cover my backside . . ."

Boolewarke laughed. "A bigot? A bigot he calls me. You tell me, Mister Johnny Simms—who isn't a bigot? Anybody whose eyes are even half-open to the world around him is going to be slanted in some direction. That is, if he's even thinking with half his head. As for covering your backside, I don't know you from Adam, and I certainly don't know how good a fighter you are. You might be dead as soon as the opening guns sound."

"Yeah, I know, stormtrooper," Simms said. "The dogs of war, the white merc in Africa may be feared by the natives, but you're not talking to some dumbass *kaffir* who believes in witch doctors."

"All right, all right," Gabriel growled. Standing, he flicked his engraved Zippo, fired up a Marlboro. "Let's not get off on the wrong foot altogether. We've got the Sword of Islam to fight, so save your energy. You want to talk politics, save it for your memoirs. Enough said."

"Not enough said. According to you, Gabe," Boolewarke said, "there might be a little engagement with the CIA on the agenda, too. There's going to come a time when I'm worried about my backside being covered. As far as our sponsors are concerned, I trust them about as far as I can spit. I'll admit, I need this chance to hang it all out there again, considering what I just left behind. But if this is a setup by the Company . . ."

"We're all thinking along the same lines, Dutch," Gabriel said. "Your concern's duly noted. You let me worry about the Company and our principal. Listen, if we're successful, I don't intend for this to be a one-shot deal. We're in it for the long run. After this, I intend for us to pick and choose our own missions, pick our own clients. As for people's backsides being covered, we roll, head-on, guns blazing. No stopping and no looking back. We gear it up, all the way, and stick together like we have to depend on each other for our lives. Because, in fact, we do have to depend on each other to make it. In battle, you know how it goes. The best defense . . ."

"Is a good offense," Simms finished. "So, what you're sayin' is that if we get the job done right, the way it should be done, nobody should have to cover anybody's backside."

"Exactly," Gabriel said. "Because you'll be leaving nothing behind but the dead."

There was a moment of silence, as each man lost himself in his own thoughts.

"A name," Dillinger grunted.

"What?" Simms asked.

Dillinger shrugged. "I was just thinking, we need a little tag to call ourselves. Y'know, like Delta Force, the SAS, the Recces. A name, yeah," the P.I. said, cracking a grin. "Something catchy for those memoirs V.G. mentioned. I don't really want to be referred to as just 'those four faceless, nameless Sad Sacks.' I kinda see this hostage recovery like we were eagles swooping to snatch up the hare. We're the eagles, and they're the hare. Only I'd like to see us drop these Arab pricks," he went on, his tone acid, "out of our claws from about ten thousand feet. A swan dive, right into the Nile maybe."

"I didn't know you were so anti-Islamic, Zac," Gabriel said, a wry grin dancing over his lips.

"I'm anti anybody who pulls the kind of chickenshit tactics this Sword of Islam has shown."

"A name, huh," Johnny Simms mused. The black pool hustler from the mean streets of D.C. stared at the fuselage wall. "I see what you're driving at, Bad One."

"Personally," Dillinger said, "I like condors—they're big and bad. But I think the damn things are almost extinct. Being named after a bird that's almost extinct couldn't do much for a man's confidence, could it?"

Simms's eyes glittered with suppressed laughter. "And the American eagle isn't an endangered species?"

The corner of his mouth twisted in a sardonic grin, Dillinger said, "What, do you think I'm a stupid cracker, Johnny-Boy?"

"Naw, just a mean, ugly one, Bad Zac."

"Now that I think a little more about it," Dillinger went on, ignoring Simms, "I like the eagle better. Noble. Strong. Courageous. Independent."

"Uh-huh," Gabriel said. "The four of us, just like eagles."

"A bloody eagle force," Boolewarke added, rubbing his square jaw.

Gabriel blew smoke. "Why not? Eagle Force, it is."

"So," Dillinger said, and picked up the G-11 caseless assault rifle, "let's go soar like eagles. Right, Dutch?"

Boolewarke grunted, glared at the P.I. for a second.

Vic Gabriel drew deeply on his cigarette. He could feel the prebattle jitters fluttering in his gut. A bad fate, he knew, awaited somebody.

Eagle Force, he thought, was about to spread its wings and swoop for the kill.

# Chapter 8

Vic Gabriel checked his Rolex. "You're late."

The ex-CIA assassin's voice boomed like rolling thunder, as it trailed away from the foothills of the Tébessa Mountain Region, across the gravel plain.

They were about sixty kilometers northwest of Kasserine and about a three-hours' drive southwest of Tunis. Jagged black plugs of ominous-looking rock, the Tébessa Mountains loomed behind the four commandos of Eagle Force. Dressed in sand-colored fatigues, the commandos were grim. Armed with assault rifles, holstered sidearms, and sheathed USMC Ka-Bars, they were ready for action.

Eyelids cracked to slits, Gabriel scoured the mountain ridge, checked the plain. Some sixth sense, honed by years of violence and treachery, warned him that someone was watching them. A late-morning sun had fired the sky to a shimmering cobalt. In the distance, about two klicks across the gravel plain, Gabriel spotted a Taureg camel caravan heading south for the oasis country where the Tunisian Sahara began. Except for the Arab nomads, Gabriel, his strike force, and Milton and his bodyguards appeared to be alone.

Moments ago, Milton's Lear Jet had touched down on the plain, taxied and parked near Black Lightning. A plume of dust, kicked up in the jet's slipstream, thinned across the plain.

Outfitted in tan khakis, tennis shoes, dark sunglasses

and a white sport shirt, Milton, surrounded by his three bodyguards, walked up the path toward Gabriel. There was a black briefcase in the mogul's hand.

Milton scowled at Gabriel. The bullet-headed bodyguard adjusted the sunglasses on his face. There was a bulge beneath the tan windbreaker each bodyguard wore. None of the four men, Gabriel thought, looked exactly happy to greet Eagle Force.

"Late? Are you forgetting just who's running this operation, Mr. Gabriel?"

"From here on out," Gabriel said, "you'd better believe I am. You may be paying the tab, but we're the ones who might have to pay the ultimate bill. I want you to meet the team, the ones who'll be dodging the lead for you, Milton. Zac Dillinger." The P.I., seated on top of a boulder, nodded curtly at Milton. "Johnny Simms." The black man, M16 canted to his shoulder, cocked a wry grin at the mogul. "Henry van Boolewarke." The Dutchman touched the brim of his Aussie bush hat, spat.

Milton studied each man for a moment. His expression appeared contemptuous. "And just what are they? Mercenaries? Assassins?"

"Eagle Force."

His expression suddenly hard, Milton looked at Dillinger. "What?"

Smiling, the P.I. shrugged. "I said, Eagle Force. You got shit in your ears, or what, Mr. Milton?"

"I hope they shoot an assault rifle as good as they shoot their mouths, Mr. Gabriel."

"Don't worry, we're not exactly a bunch of snot-nosed schoolkids, Milt," Dillinger remarked.

"Uh-huh. Here," the mogul said, and gave Gabriel the briefcase. "The ransom money. There's a couple of things you need to know first."

"How come I don't like the sound of that?" Gabriel said.

"One: there's only two million in the briefcase."

Gabriel peered at Milton. "What?"

Milton handed Gabriel a slip of paper. "There's the address in Tunis where you are to meet a delegation being sent by your target, Hammadi."

"A delegation?" Simms scoffed. "You make it sound like we're just going to shoot the bull with some UN flunkies."

Milton ignored the black man. "After landing at the Tunis–Carthage International Airport, you will proceed immediately to that address."

"What about transportation?" Gabriel asked.

"They have cabs in Tunis."

"You expect us to load up enough firepower to arm the French Foreign Legion and pile it in a cab?" Gabriel growled.

An odd smile from Milton. He handed Gabriel another slip of paper. "An address just outside the airport where you can pick up a Land Rover."

Gabriel, believing Milton was jerking him around, was beginning to feel mean and ugly. "Why only half the money?"

"The amount is unimportant. It isn't real anyway."

Now Gabriel was hot. He started to unlatch the briefcase, but Milton barked, "Don't open it! It's rigged with plastic explosives."

Shaking his head, Johnny Simms muttered an oath. "Phony money. A briefcase set to blow up in our faces. The Muzzies'll hand us our heads before we ever get outta Tunis if they know that money ain't real."

"How do we know *our* money isn't counterfeit either, Milton?" Dillinger asked.

"It's real," Milton answered.

"What am I supposed to tell this big delegation when they want to open the briefcase?" Gabriel wanted to know.

"Tell them the truth: only I know how to deactivate the explosives. But we shouldn't have to get that far, should we, Mr. Gabriel? Once Pamela's been delivered, the rest of your money . . ."

"Yeah, yeah," Gabriel growled, "I know the routine. Save the tears and the speech for the reunion." Gabriel pulled a miniature black box out of his pants pocket. He flicked a switch and a red light flashed on the box.

"What's that?" Milton asked.

"A homing device," Gabriel answered. "With all the new angles of the dangle you're throwing at me, you don't want me to get lost, do you, Milt?"

Jaw clenched, Milton drew a deep breath, exhaled loudly. "I'm sure you won't get lost when it comes time to collect your money."

"You got that right," Dillinger said. "I've already got it spent, Milt. I'm taking a body count in my head now."

"You won't be able to spend anything," one of Milton's bodyguards retorted, "if you're dead."

"These old warbones, Magilla Gorilla, have seen more action than a dozen Charles Bronson movies. You'll be seeing my ugly mug again, count on it."

Ignoring Dillinger, Milton asked Gabriel, "So, I can trust you to do the job from here on out?"

"What do you think, Mr. Milton?"


"What do you think, Mr. Sprenger?"

The high-powered camera clicked four times in Torquemada's hands.

Crouched behind a boulder along the ridge of a high hill, Sprenger and Torquemada were two hundred meters south of the conference.

The Traq 10 × 40 binos lowered away from Sprenger's eyes. Squinting, he held his gaze on the men to his far left. "What did our friend Albert Speer once say about the anti-Christ, Adolf Hitler?" Sprenger posed.

"He said, and I quote, '*One seldom recognizes the devil*

83

*when he is putting his hand on your shoulder.'* So, just who here is playing the role of the devil?"

"All of us. And maybe none of us," Sprenger answered. Our hand is on Milton's shoulder, and Milton's hand is on Gabriel's shoulder."

"And Target Gabriel," Torquemada added, "has just signed a pact with the devil."

"We proceed at once to the village. The chopper's waiting. According to friend Milton, the meet goes down in Tunis."

"Probe?"

"Probe. Wait and watch. Perhaps . . . well, whoever these three men are . . . we'll run it down when we get back."

"Will the Company use them, do you think?"

"Use, perhaps. Discard, most definitely. Remember, Gabriel is the key here. As quickly as he found those other commandos—I assume he's had something in mind for some time now."

"So, he's forgotten Saunders?"

"Doubtful. Nobody's forgotten Michael Saunders. And nobody . . . nobody is about to forget Vic Gabriel."

Torquemada nodded. "Not until the worms are eating the flesh off his bones."

*"Vietnam, son, is only the tip of the iceberg."*
*Twenty-year-old Second Lieutenant Vic Gabriel of the 7th SFG tried to shut out the whapping bleat of the Huey UH-1D's rotors as the chopper lowered for the LZ, ten klicks east of Chu Lai. With effort, he mentally focused in on his father's voice. Tip of the iceberg? Just what did his father mean by that? He was three months into his second tour in Vietnam, and he still wondered if his father was implying that this dirty little war was some stepping-stone to a great holocaust. But, of course, there was some deeper meaning to what his father had said. There always was.*

*Mankind, his father had said, is headed into its most perilous and terrible time yet. A deeply religious man, his father had told him to read and re-read the Book of Revelation. The signs are all around, one just has to look to be able to see them. So, if the Vietnam war was merely a shadow of some conflict that was to spread across Asia, and perhaps around the world, then Vic Gabriel wasn't sure if he wanted any part of it. Then again, he might not have any choice. The average age of a GI in Vietnam was nineteen. Teenagers. Kids. Hell, babies, really. Cherries they were called before they got their first taste of first blood in this green jungle hell. But, faced with death day in and day out, Vic Gabriel had seen that a boy-man becomes a man, hell, an old man before long—before his time. He'd seen his buddies fall victim to more than one VC bullet or booby trap. And he'd seen guys in his detachment left for worse than dead. The really unlucky ones, he'd decided, were the guys who got an arm or a leg, or two arms and two legs, blown off by a mine. Survival became a soldier's top priority.*

*But just surviving didn't win a war. As frightened as he'd been on that first walk in the sun, hunting down VC on a search-and-destroy, Vic Gabriel had learned that your best chances at surviving were to fight. Fight with a vengeance. Strike first. Strike hard. Strike last. Don't think about losing that arm or leg. Don't think about dying. Just put your nose right there in the battle, and let it rip. And remember, your buddies are just as scared as you are. Combat really did prove the man, he'd seen. Heroes and cowards. And all shades in between. But a man, his father had long ago told him, faced his fear, confronted it, and acted. He didn't let the fear paralyze him into doing nothing. Luckily for Vic Gabriel, those years of training in the Colorado wilderness as a boy had paid off. The combat survival training. Using and stripping down, blindfolded, weapons, ranging from a .45 Colt to an M-14 to .50 caliber machine guns. The long hours of rigorous physical condi-*

*tioning. The runs through obstacle courses, under fire, learning combat tactics and maneuvers. Knife-fighting. Sniping. The long winter months when his father would send him out into the wilderness, alone, with nothing but his bare hands and his knowledge, in theory, of surviving off the land. Sure, the training had paid off—it seemed. Except that back then, there was no enemy to face down in a life-or-death confrontation.*

*Now, Vic Gabriel was putting the theories into practice. And, yeah, he realized, that was really the only way to learn. Here, against the Vietcong, you didn't get a second chance to make the same mistake.*

*Second Lieutenant Vic Gabriel felt the jolt as the slick touched down. For a second, he looked at his Vietcong prisoner, the last of four prisoners being transported from Special Detachment Camp Y for interrogation. Operation Mudslide had been anything but a success in Vic Gabriel's mind. Fifteen dead cong. And four surviving VC, who had been flushed out of their hole and captured after three days of hand-to-hand fighting. Dug out by grenades and flame-throwers. Sorrow stabbed Vic Gabriel. Four American dead, four young men, he thought. . . . Damn, but he didn't even want to think about it. He couldn't think about it. He'd already been wounded twice in combat, and the second bullet had missed his heart by a fraction of an inch. He was alive, had survived again, when others had died. And he'd known those dead men. All of them. Warriors who had gone into the fight without flinching, without complaint. Grim. Determined. Maybe they hadn't wanted to be there, but who did? Now they were going home, all right. Home for good. And what about their families, their girlfriends? It just didn't make any sense. Didn't really make one goddamn bit of sense.*

*M16 in hand, Gabriel escorted his prisoner out of the chopper. Disembarking, the rotor wash pounding over him, he pushed through the elephant grass, heading toward the tent near the edge of the jungle treeline. Like a furnace, the sun beat down on his neck. It was either hot or poured down rain in Vietnam. No in-betweens. A soldier became adjusted to discomfort quickly. The insects and leeches, the poisonous snakes, the marches through the jungle and the swamps . . . yeah, you got used to it, all right. Vic Gabriel thought it strange how a man can adapt so easily to such a hostile environment. Adjust, then harden himself even to the sight of violent death.*

*Sweeping aside the flap to the tent, Vic Gabriel ushered his prisoner inside. His father was there waiting for him. So was the CIA man who had been instrumental in melding father and son into something else. The "Special Project," the CIA called them. The father and son killteam. Used for penetrations into Laos and Cambodia to hunt down and execute Vietcong officers on the Company hit list. The Special Forces Top Secret Dynamic Duo, they were called.*

*"All right, that's the last of them. Good. Let's get on with this."*

*Michael Saunders had a cold voice, a brutal face that both fascinated Vic Gabriel and made him slightly wary of the man. Saunders was tall, broad, with cold blue eyes that seemed like a chip right out of a block of ice. Decked out in tiger-striped camous, he even seemed to move with the grace of a jungle cat. And Saunders, another one of those CIA shadow men who seemed to be lurking around everywhere in Vietnam, almost always had his hand wrapped around his .45 Colt, as if he was itching to unleather that gun and fire away. Just for the hell of it, Vic Gabriel decided. Saunders seemed like the type. Cold-blooded. Sadistic even. There was a glint in the operative's eyes, something close to laughter, that Vic Gabriel didn't trust. His father, he knew, didn't care too much for Saunders either.*

*It was then that Vic Gabriel sensed the tension, and, as he turned his prisoner over to Saunders, he felt as if he were walking on brittle ice. The other three VC prisoners, their hands roped behind their backs, were sitting on the ground. Their faces were puffy and bruised, slicked with blood. Then Vic Gabriel noticed the young Vietnamese girl. She had to be all of thirteen or fourteen. Long black hair. Almond skin. Oval face. She was pretty, but the terror, no, the hatred in her eyes made her appear less than attractive. Vic Gabriel tried to read into her eyes, but she just stared back at him in defiance, that calm but steely gaze he'd seen so many times in the eyes of Vietnamese. He wondered what she was doing there for the interrogation. He had to assume she was a tool, an instrument to be used by Saunders to pry information out of the other prisoners.*

*Saunders focused grim attention on one of the Viet-cong men, exhaled a weary sigh as he moved to stand beside the prisoner. "Okay, Charlie, I've played around with you long enough, you slant-eyed shit. I'm going to ask the same questions once more, but this time I want answers. Last time, last chance. You've taken some of our people prisoner—and God only knows what you've done to them. Where are they?"*

*The prisoner spat at Saunders's feet.*

*Vic stood next to his father. There was a hint of anger in the Colonel's eyes. The Colonel, his own M16 canted against a small wooden chair, flicked a Zippo and fired up a cigarette. Vic looked at his father for a moment, but the Colonel just stared at the back of Saunders's head.*

*Suddenly, some uncontrollable rage seized Saunders. In less time than it takes to blink an eye, the .45 Colt leapt from Saunders's holster and cannoned a round. The retort of gunfire sounded like a grenade blast in the close confines of the tent to Vic Gabriel. The slug drilled through the VC's ear. Blood burst out the other side of his shattered skull, spraying the girl's face. Vic Gabriel was shocked by the senseless brutality of such an act, felt as if his feet were rooted to the ground. The dead VC seemed to topple into the girl's lap in slow motion. But Vic's father moved like a wink of lightning, and the M16 was in the Colonel's hands*

88

and aimed at Saunders before the CIA man could turn his
.45 on the girl, who looked at the killer with depthless
hatred.

"I figured you the type to do something like that,
Saunders."

His father's voice was measured, and there was steel in
that voice. Vic Gabriel knew his father was a split-second
away from gunning Saunders down.

"What the fuck are you talking about, Colonel?"

"I've stood by for the better part of an hour, and
watched you beat these prisoners to a pulp. I've seen
enough. That's what I'm talking about. This isn't exactly
what I thought you had in mind for an interrogation.
Cold-blooded murder just doesn't go right for me."

"Cold-blooded murder? Jesus Christ, open your fuckin' eyes, Colonel. Where the hell do you think you are?
Back in the bosom of the World?" Saunders glanced down
at the corpse with contempt. "You think Charlie's treating
our people any better?"

"If they aren't, then that makes them that much worse,
right?"

Saunders stared at the Colonel for a long moment,
seemed to weigh his next words carefully.

"Let me tell you something, Colonel, unless you haven't
noticed we brought you and your son in on this to do a job.
That was to bring back targeted VC to us. You turn them
over to us. You let us do the rest. I'm not interested in any
bright-eyed, bleeding heart morality from you. I've got a
job to do. Your job is done. You're Company property at
the moment, and you're taking orders from me. If it weren't
for me, there wouldn't be any 'Special Project,' no hotshot
father-and-son team. You wanna play Captain Marvel,
save it for your memoirs after the war, all right. I don't
have time for your bullshit, soldier."

"Murdering these prisoners isn't going to get our
people back, Saunders. Just what were you planning to do
next? Kill the girl?"

"If that's what it takes."

"Forget it, Saunders. You do that, I'll kill you, as sure as I'm standing here."

Saunders looked at the Colonel in disbelief, then anger. "What did you say, mister?"

"You heard me."

"Yeah, I heard you, all right. Okay, Colonel," he said, then holstered his .45. "Have it your way. But I'll remember this. While you piss around with these prisoners, just remember—our people are being tortured somewhere, even dying right at this moment. And you, Colonel, yeah, you, you will have killed them. All because you're going to stand there and threaten to blow my guts out my stomach over some fuckin' gooks who wouldn't think twice about doing to you what I just did to that," he said, again looking down at the dead VC.

"Hey, I'm not going to interfere unless what I see isn't going to get any results. Go ahead with your interrogation, Saunders. But no more killing like that. You read me?"

"Yeah, I read you. Loud and clear, Colonel." Saunders's gaze narrowed. "But I'll remember this. And, you'll regret it. Believe me."

The Colonel lowered his M16. He stood in cold silence.

Vic Gabriel felt like a spectator. But there was a time-bomb ticking away inside of him, and he was ready to act on his father's behalf if Saunders went for his gun. Michael Saunders, he suspected, wasn't a man to be put down and made to back off by anybody. His father, Vic Gabriel sensed, had just stepped over some line Saunders kept drawn between himself and his enemies.

Something warned Vic Gabriel that this day would come back to haunt him.

Vietnam may just well be the tip of an iceberg, after all.

The flames raged. A whirlwind of fire swirled, incinerating the large one-story building.

Muhmad Hammadi smiled. He heard the hiss of fire in the distance. His shock troops were preparing for their holy mission. For as long as he could remember, Hammadi had been fascinated by fire. Fire cleansed, purified. Fire was the most fearsome element on earth. Fire was a tool. A tool, yes, to be turned into a weapon. Hammadi had at least twenty of the ultimate weapons at his disposal. Flame-throwers.

Turning, his hand fisted over the bejeweled hilt of his *jambiya*, Hammadi rested a dark stare on his hostages. Five men. All Americans. All Western imperialist whores for the Great Satan. Hammadi smiled, but the smile didn't reach his eyes. When he got what he wanted from Bradley Milton, the hostages would all die. There could be no mercy shown to the devils.

With five million dollars' worth of American money, Hammadi would have very little trouble rounding up an even stronger following in the Arab freedom fighter underworld. Syria. Libya. Jordan. Palestine. Lebanon. It didn't matter where the holy warriors came from; their cause, whether they were Shiite or Sunni, was the same. Vengeance against the oppressors of Islam, that was all that mattered, that was all that was holy to Hammadi. Before he'd given his life over to Allah, Hammadi had long since vowed that the Zionist dagger of Israel would be removed from the side of Arab unity forever, that terrorism would be imported on an apocalyptic scale to the United States, and that the Bekaa Valley would belong to a Greater Syria that would be recognized as the most powerful of all the Arab states. If the world believed a ring of fire now encircled the Middle East, well, Hammadi determined, the world had tasted nothing yet of Islamic wrath. It was fitting, Hammadi decided, as he looked around at the fertile valley, gazed at the forests of oak, pine, and juniper blanketing the hills that surrounded the Sword of Islam compound, that Tunisia would be the Arab country that would soon be exporting vengeance and terror and death against the infidel enslavers. More than twenty years ago, Tunisia had enraged the Arab states by telling them they might as well recognize Israel's existence. As surely as Muhammad was the one, the true Prophet, ancient Carthage would taste its own blood again. Soon. Very soon. And who would stop the Sword of Islam? The West appeared impotent in the face of the *jihad's* onslaught. And Russia? The Soviets were merely standing by in the shadows, laughing, encouraging the Islamic freedom fighters in their holy war against the West, even though the Russians didn't believe anything was holy except for communism.

No one, Hammadi believed, could stop him. No one had the strength to defeat him. Certainly, no one had the courage to stand up to his army of freedom fighters, a determined and savage horde that would fight to the death, go down to the last warrior. And Hannibal, he joked to himself, was long since dead, had tackled the stubborn, fierce Romans one time too many.

Tunisia was a land won and lost, time and again. The Phoenicians had come and gone in Tunisia, but they had left their ghosts behind in the Berbers. The Romans had conquered the land and lost their empire to the Vandals, who grew soft and lazy in the warm climate of Tunisia. The Byzantines, the Turks, the French—they'd all come to Tunisia, won their claims to the timeless land only to lose their hold eventually and vanish into the pages of history books. But the Sword of Islam would stay, and Tunisia would be the nerve center of renewed Islamic conquest.

Yes, Hammadi was prepared to begin a crusade. He was prepared to conquer, even if that meant slaughtering the unfaithful by the thousands. By the tens of thousands. First, Hammadi had to secure the ransom money from Bradley Milton. Once he had the money, Hammadi would go to the Soviets and buy as much firepower as he could. Hammadi detested the atheistic, obnoxious Soviets, but he would have the final laugh on the Russians. With their own weapons, Hammadi and his shock troops were going to kill

Russians. Lots of Russians. Important Russians. In less than a month, an arms talk between the Superpowers was set to take place in Geneva. The Russians were the primary targets. By executing the Soviet delegation, Hammadi hoped a permanent wedge would be driven between East and West. It might not start a war between the Superpowers, Hammadi realized, but he at least intended to fan the flames of hostility and suspicion between the two great evil states of the world.

The hostages, flanked by six AK-47-toting Arabs, stood before the white-washed walls of Hammadi's command post. As Hammadi looked around at the valley, the hostages stared at him in terror, as if he was a madman. Hammadi turned grim attention on the hostages. The time had come, he decided, to inject horror, real horror, into the hearts of his captives.

"You." Hammadi smiled as he looked at the hostage who was called Benjamin Toukheim. A Jewish doctor from Long Island, Toukheim had been kidnapped from his French villa more than two months ago by Hammadi's shock troops. Hammadi's hit team had slain Toukheim's wife and twenty-year-old daughter, hung them upside-down from the rafters in the living room of the villa. Toukheim was a rich Jew, a pig, Hammadi thought. Most likely, Hammadi decided, the good doctor had lied and cheated his way to the top, and money to Toukheim was probably much more important than saving lives. The Jew doctor, Hammadi decided, would make a fitting example.

Hatred burned in Toukheim's eyes, his lower lip quivering. Hammadi read the pain and torment in Toukheim's eyes. The memories of what he'd seen in France, Hammadi knew, inflamed Toukheim's heart with vengeance. Hammadi felt strong. The Syrian knew how to turn a man's hatred against himself. One gets the upper hand on the enemy, Hammadi believed, then goads that enemy until a nerve is touched off. With the upper hand, one then comes down on the enemy and crushes him like a bug.

"Perhaps you hate my stinking Syrian guts, doctor?" Toukheim trembled with rage.

"I can see you are having great difficulty controlling your emotions, my good doctor."

"You murdering bastard!" Toukheim shouted. Hands curled like claws, the doctor charged Hammadi. The butt of an AK-47 chopped over Toukheim's head. Face-first, Toukheim hit the earth. The *Sadi* soldier who had dropped Toukheim drove a boot into the doctor's ribs.

Hammadi felt his hatred for Jews overpowering him. It was obvious, he believed, that the Jews were a race who were damned to suffering for all time. They were greedy and cutthroat and believed themselves superior. They had stolen land that rightfully belonged to Arabs. Bending, fisting a handful of Toukheim's hair and wrenching his face up, Hammadi wanted to cut the Jew's throat open with his *jambiya*. But a more fitting example had already been arranged.

"Stand up, stand up, you dog!" Hammadi hissed, pulling Toukheim to his feet by the hair. Snaking the *jambiya* from inside the black sash fastened around his khakis, Hammadi pressed the tip of the blade against Toukheim's throat.

"Kill me. Kill me. Just like you did my wife and daughter."

Hammadi laughed.

"You think you and your murderers are holy warriors fighting your *jihad*?" Toukheim rasped. "You murderers of innocent women and children! You have no real backbone. You have no chutzpah."

Hammadi lowered the Arab fighting knife by his side, nodded. "We will see, good doctor, who has balls. Come with me. Bring the others!" he ordered his soldiers.

Hammadi, his hand digging into Toukheim's shoulder, hauled the doctor away from the command post. Moments later, Hammadi stopped, stood with Toukheim between two long rows of white-washed quarters that housed his soldiers.

"Listen to me, you men," Hammadi addressed the hostages. "I have been accused of having no balls by this Jew dog. But I am a fair man, a reasonable man. I am a man of Allah, and I believe in justice. At this moment, I am prepared to show you justice. I am letting the good doctor run for his life."

Fear shadowed Toukheim's face as Hammadi released the doctor. A bead of sweat dripped off the doctor's sun-cracked lips. His Adam's apple bobbed as he swallowed hard.

Hammadi looked Toukheim dead in the eye. "You have thirty seconds before my men fire on you. Run." Toukheim held his ground. "Run!"

Shaking in terror and hatred, Toukheim stumbled away from Hammadi. Then, without looking back, Toukheim ran.

Hammadi turned. Hands on his hips, he watched as Toukheim sprinted between the barracks.

The doctor's heels kicked up puffs of dust.

A smile slit Hammadi's lips.

The Sword of Islam soldiers raised their AK-47s.

"No!" one of the hostages yelled, before the barrel of an assault rifle cracked him in the face.

Autofire ripped the air.

Bullets stitching the ground behind him, Toukheim nose-dived to the dirt.

"Run! Or die!" Hammadi screamed at Toukheim.

Autofire drilling a tracking line of fire behind him, Toukheim bolted to his feet. He sprinted past the end of the barracks.

Hammadi's laughter rang down the narrow gap between the barracks.

A tongue of fire whooshed.

Shrieking.

A hostage cursed.

The stream of fire continued to wash over Toukheim. Flailing on the ground, Toukheim's blood-curdling screams seemed suspended in the air, a palpable force. The dragon's spray of fire hissed, on and on, pinning the human torch to the earth. Finally, the tail of flames ceased to exist. The screaming ended, too. Beneath the wave of fire, Toukheim was incinerated into a shriveled black mummy.

Slowly, the stench of melting flesh stinging his senses, Hammadi walked toward the flames. The world was now cleaner, Hammadi thought, purified of the existence of another Jew. Silently, Hammadi gave glory to Allah.

Closing down on the human torch, Hammadi stopped.

Pamela Milton walked up to Hammadi. She held the nozzle of the flamethrower in her hands, the silvery pack strapped to her back. Behind the woman, flames towered into the sky.

For a long moment, Hammadi looked deep into the woman's blue eyes. Her eyes were clear, but they glinted with a madness not even he was sure he understood. She was beautiful. She belonged to one of Hammadi's soldiers, Hamil el Bejin, but even so, Hammadi had already taken her body—many times. Bejin might own her heart and soul, Hammadi thought, but the whore's body belonged to him.

"You are quite capable with that," Hammadi said, holding the woman's stare. "He was an enemy."

"Then he deserved death. Perhaps, as you have said before, there is justice in the world, after all."

Hammadi nodded. "Your father is an enemy, also. Would you do the same to him?"

"My father is a pig." Her voice turned cold, her gaze hard. "I would kill him, yes, if I had to. I'm not the spoiled little rich brat that you think I am, Muhmad. I have proven my loyalty to you many times already."

Hammadi pursed his lips. "I never said you were a spoiled little rich brat," he told her, but thought, *You are a slut, a tool to be used. Your money had bought you everything you ever wanted. You are worse than spoiled. You are a traitor to your own. You are pathetic.*

"I have not seen Hamil this morning. Where is he?"

"He was sent to Carthage," Hammadi answered. "Your father is delivering the ransom money there. Which brings us to another problem."

"Problem?"

"How loyal are you to the cause?"

Bitterness flared into the woman's eyes. "I have given my life over to the cause. I have left my father and all of his riches. I have left America to fight by your side. To the death, if necessary."

"So you say."

"So I mean."

"Understand that your father must be killed once the money is delivered." Hammadi looked at his lover, saw fear and a flicker of regret in her eyes. "You will go to him. You will kill him. It is the only thing that can be done." Now Hammadi saw indecision. "Is that a problem?"

Pamela Milton was silent for a moment. "No."

"Very well. Meet me in my headquarters in one hour. We will discuss the execution in further detail there."

Wheeling, Hammadi left the woman alone beside the barracks. There would be no "discussion." Hammadi smiled to himself, ignoring the fierce hatred in the eyes of the hostages. He would strip the Western slut naked, pin her to the floor, and take her body. That was their "discussion." It was Allah's Will. What now belonged to the enemies would soon be handed over in the spoils of war to the Sword of Islam. Wealth. Power. Even their women.

Pamela Milton watched Hammadi as he brushed past the hostages. There was a haunted look in her eyes suddenly. Then, staring down at the human pyre beside her, Pamela Milton's expression changed to savage determination.

# Chapter 9

The past can be the key to the future. History does repeat itself, Vic Gabriel believed, unless a man learns from his mistakes. And unless he missed his guess altogether, Gabriel's past involvement with the CIA would be coming back to haunt him. More than once, since his days with Special Forces in Vietnam, where he'd fought alongside his father, Gabriel had quit the Company. Sooner or later, Gabriel knew, he would have to face the music. A dance of death with assassins from the Company's Special Operations Division was in the future.

And the future was appearing blacker as the hours mounted.

Sure, Gabriel admitted to himself, there was more than one reason why he'd accepted Milton's contract for slaughter. And one of those reasons was vengeance. Since Milton had been guided to him by the Company, Gabriel knew the CIA wanted something. Or someone. And that someone was most likely Michael Saunders. The Company wanted Saunders because he had defected to the KGB after the brutal affair in Paris. So Paris had determined Vic Gabriel's future in more ways than one. It was in Paris, too, that Gabriel's father had been murdered during a Company-sponsored hit on Syrian terrorists who had taken the American embassy hostage—murdered by Saunders. And since that day, Gabriel had wanted nothing less than Saunders's head. The past would not release Vic Gabriel.

Indeed, Gabriel thought, memory may fade with time, but the past will always live—the mistakes we have made, our oversights lay the ground rules for our present struggles.

"Jasmine! Gold! Four dinars only two hundred millimes! Jasmine! The scent alone will kill all germs! Trust Rashif!"

Togged in black, Vic Gabriel crossed the Avenue du Président Habib Bourguiba. Angling a block away from Martyrs Square, he passed beneath a sculpted sandstone arch. Moving down a narrow stone-stepped street, Gabriel entered still another vaulted *suq* bustling with headclothed Arab vendors hawking their wares. Air sweet with perfume. More hustling of cheap goods.

The briefcase with the counterfeit two million American dollars in hand, Gabriel knew he was literally a walking time bomb. With nothing but grim determination and the Detonics .45 "Combat Master" Mark VI in a shoulder rig beneath his black windbreaker, Gabriel admitted to himself that he was a little nervous about his meet with the Arab fanatics. Sometimes savagery and guts wasn't enough. There was no telling what the terrorists would do when they were told the briefcase was rigged to blow up if opened. Hell, they might even think they were being lied to or, worse, set up to take a nose dive into death.

Slaughtering the Sword of Islam fanatics was precisely what Gabriel intended to do, damn right. But it would help, he thought, if he could dictate the terms of engagement. Even though he knew full well that in the heat of battle Lady Luck didn't smile on anybody. Bullets cared nothing about right or wrong. Only the quickest, meanest, most determined side wins. Sure, in every battle there were accidents and unforeseen opportunities—*but careful planning and determined execution almost always tipped the scales of fortune*. Almost always. There was always a human factor involved—and here it was whether or not the Sword of Islam fanatics believed Gabriel was telling the truth about the briefcase.

Turning, Gabriel spotted his backup. Dressed in black robes, their heads wrapped in *kaffiyahs*, Dillinger, Simms, and Boolewarke trailed Gabriel by a dozen meters. Cover. A black Berber walking the streets of Tunis might be a little suspect, so Johnny Simms kept the scarf across his face; only the black man's eyes showed above the scarf. In the oppressive heat, Gabriel knew his troops were sweltering in their grab, but losing sweat was always better than losing blood. Beneath their robes, each commando toted a mini-Uzi and a Ka-Bar fighting knife. Gabriel hoped that amount of firepower and steel would be enough if the meet soured, erupted into a bloody confrontation. Their Land Rover was parked on the outskirts of Tunis. Because they didn't know the city and because, besides, the narrow streets and countless, endless alleyways made driving in Tunis an impossibility, the Land Rover would stay where it was until it was needed.

Gabriel faced front, kept moving. He was in the Kasba area of Tunis Medina. Even though this was his first time in Tunis, Gabriel still liked to think of the ancient city as Carthage. To Gabriel, tradition equaled culture, and culture meant a people had pride in themselves and their history, a sense of their own uniqueness among the human race. Power had changed hands many times in Carthage, from the first Phoenician colony around 850 B.C. until the Romans laid waste to the city and plowed salt into the land in 146 B.C. But the city, indeed the land and its people, endured. They sat at the edge of time. After all, Gabriel thought, wasn't civilization born at the edges of North Africa?

With the address of the meeting memorized, Gabriel swiftly moved through the *suqs*. Bright carpets, jebbas, cheap oriental bric-a-bric, Arab zodiac plaques, and brassware jammed the stalls in the market place. Jewelry shops sparkled in the sunlight. Each vendor tried to outshout the other for the attention of passersby. Mistaking Gabriel for a foreigner of easy pickings, Arabs thrust gold necklaces at

Gabriel. The ex-CIA assassin kept moving. Gabriel pretended to ignore the hustle around him, but he was aware of every movement, counting on his well-honed sixth sense for danger to cover his backside. Ragged barefoot urchins, laughing and shouting, eyeing the briefcase in Gabriel's hand. Veiled women brushing by the American, keeping their billowy white *sefsaris* close to their faces but trying to make eye contact with the tall man in black. If someone attempted to snatch the briefcase out of his hand, Gabriel would have to shoot that person dead. There was no time to be running around Tunis, chasing a thief down alleys that led into the unknown.

Sparrows fluttered in the shadows of narrow passageways, and Gabriel felt the jolt of his own edginess. From the minaret of a mosque beyond the *suqs*, Gabriel heard the faithful calls to Allah. What had not too long ago been French Protectorate Tunis was a tightly packed medieval-looking city, crammed with *suqs*, mosques, the chambered-courtyards called *zawias* in Arabic, and ornately arched doorways. The enemy could have been any one of hundreds of Arabs on the streets.

Rounding the corner, Gabriel moved away from the *suqs*. Suddenly, Gabriel felt the muzzle of a pistol jabbing against his spine. Good sense warned him not to turn around. Gut instinct told him he had found a member of the Sword of Islam delegation.

"Is this a stickup, pal?"

Silence.

"*Enti beteet-kal-limi engelizee?*"

"Of course, I speak English. Keep moving. And don't turn around."

Gabriel did as he was ordered.

"Is the money in the briefcase?"

"Yeah. But we've got a little problem, Abdul."

*Death had dealt its hardest blow to Vic Gabriel. Fate could indeed be cruel.*

*But man could be worse.*

*It had been three days since he'd received the news, and he was still numb with disbelief. With grief and rage.*

*The rescue mission to free the American hostages held by Syrian terrorists at the embassy in Paris had been a total disaster. A wipeout, a snafu. Once again, the terrorists had smeared shit all over Uncle Sam's face.*

*But that was only the half of it. And far from the worst of it as far as Vic Gabriel was concerned.*

*Colonel Charles Gabriel had been killed while storming the embassy with a crack team of hand-picked commandos. Murdered, to be more exact. According to the man from the CIA, the errand boy from Langley who had given Vic Gabriel the tragic news at his home in Fairfax, Virginia, his father had not died from the bullets from the gun of a mad dog terrorist. No, the killer had been one Michael Saunders.*

*The shadow man from the Vietnam days. The creator of that famous "Special Project," the father-son killteam. The behind-enemy-lines duo who had penetrated into Laos and Cambodia repeatedly to assassinate select Vietcong targets. Saunders. Butcher. Traitor. Apparently, Saunders was now connected with the KGB. And, as usual, Moscow had found a way to use a terrorist incident to their advantage. Saunders had defected, but not even the CIA was sure why he'd gone "over the wall." Vic Gabriel could only guess as to why Saunders had turned traitor, too. He was well aware of the long-running animosity between his father and Saunders. Saunders, the brutal, sadistic Company shadow man who believed that his word and his will were equal to God's, a man who would just as soon shoot a VC prisoner in the head as interrogate him. Colonel Gabriel, the soldier, warrior, hero, man of wisdom and compassion. A man who knew the sides, and always chose the right one. A man who could play the long odds because he had guts and integrity. The father Vic had loved and admired. The father who had given him guidance and direction, instilled values in him and taught him respect for life. The father, now dead and gone. But why? What had happened? Why, why, why? Goddammit, why!? Had Saunders been motivated by vengeance? Greed? Whatever the reason, Vic Gabriel would hunt the bastard down and find out. Then, he'd drop Saunders where he stood. And, no, he wouldn't shoot Saunders in the back like the bastard had done to his father. He'd do it, face-to-face, staring into Saunders's eyes before he punched his ticket to hell.*

*But there was something that needed to be done first. Something Vic Gabriel had waited a long, long time to do. He hadn't seen his brother since before his first tour of duty in Vietnam.*

*Now, he wanted to break the news to his brother personally. Jim Gabriel, the draft dodger who had sat out the Vietnam war in Canada. Jim Gabriel, who was now a big cocaine dealer around the streets of Washington, D.C., and its suburbs. Jim Gabriel, the big bagman. Big fucking deal.*

*The apartment complex was just inside the Maryland line, on the outskirts of D.C. The old brick-front buildings were seedy-looking, and Gabriel could smell the futility and desperation in the air almost as strong as the stench of urine and trash around the stoops and the dark crevices between the buildings. The places where the crack deals went down. The places where the demons of drug addiction dwelled.*

*As he stepped down the sidewalk, checking the buildings for the correct address, he wondered if his brother even knew about their father's death. Wondered if Jim even really cared about Dad.*

*It wasn't that hard tracking his brother down. Everybody in town seemed to know Jim Gabriel, big crackman, big wheeler and dealer in rock cocaine. People in the drug trade were more willing to talk when a .45 automatic was pressed up against their nose. That .45 was now holstered beneath Vic Gabriel's white windbreaker.*

Ascending the steps to the target building, Gabriel unzipped his windbreaker. He closed down on the door. He'd come as the bearer of bad new, and if anybody got in his way he'd become the angel of death. In one hell of a hurry.

With a thunderous kick from the heel of his combat boot, Gabriel sent the door crashing against the wall. The .45 Colt was drawn and tracking. The living room became a hive of chaos.

And death entered the crackhouse.

A black hulk leapt off the sofa. Through a cloud of drifting white smoke, Gabriel saw that guy reach for an Uzi submachine gun.

The .45 boomed.

A podburst of gore and muck exploded out the back of the black hulk's skull. Slamming off the wall, the black hulk hammered down on a coffee table littered with plastic packets, his bulk crushing glass pipes to slivers.

Three other figures in that room froze. One of them was Jim Gabriel.

"V-Vic . . . what . . . what . . ."

"My question exactly . . . brother. What?"

Grim-faced, Gabriel moved across the room, the muzzle of his .45 trained, rocksteady, on the blacks. The two blacks in front of the stove with the vials of cooked cocaine in their hands looked at Gabriel, and he read the play in their eyes.

"Don't flinch. Don't even fart, dudes," Gabriel growled. "Anybody else here?"

The blacks hesitated, but Jim Gabriel said, "No."

"If you lie, you die. I think you understand that kind of street talk, brother."

Suddenly, there was contempt in Jim Gabriel's eyes. Suddenly, he seemed smug and arrogant.

"Looks like you just couldn't get the killing out of your blood, huh, big brother. What's the matter? There weren't enough babies over there in Nam to kill."

Vic Gabriel bit down on his rage. He couldn't believe his brother would talk like that to him. But then again, he wasn't that surprised either. Jim never had any character. You can't step on something with no spine and expect to break its back.

Vic Gabriel hit his brother with the news. "Dad's dead."

When his brother cocked a half-smile at him, Vic Gabriel was tempted to cross the distance between them and break his face in half.

"That's it," Vic Gabriel growled. "You're just going to stand there and smile?"

"What do you want me to do, big brother? Break down and shed tears of blood for the old man? Me, the loser. The little brother who couldn't even keep pace with you in a five-mile run. Little brother, the quitter. You were always his fair-haired boy. You could do no wrong. You're the big war hero now, remember? I'm just a piece-of-shit lowlife, dealing dope."

"You are what you want to be, little brother. You know what your problem is, Jim? You always just felt sorry for yourself, Jim. You never tried, Jim. You always gave up too easily."

"Bullshit! Hey, man, maybe you never stopped to consider me, huh? Maybe I'm just not as good as you. Maybe I'd lose before I ever even tried. Think about it."

"I have."

"Bullshit."

"Bullshit, all you want. I'm going. Dad's dead. I thought you might want to know."

"Well, thanks for letting me know. Big brother . . . asshole."

And Vic Gabriel left his brother standing there in that kitchen. Jim Gabriel. Hating their father. Hating his older brother. But really hating himself. Knowing he was wrong but doing nothing to try to make himself right.

*Vic Gabriel felt disgust. And for just a second, he felt defeat. Despair.*

*Dad had been right all along.*

*Jim had come to a bad end. A bad end that would lead him right to a dead end.*

*And death.*

*Vic Gabriel walked out of that damn place. It stunk. It reeked of human waste. Of spiritual death.*

*For just a second, Vic Gabriel felt the tears threatening to burn themselves into the corners of his eyes.*

*He sucked it up. He had to be strong. Someone had to be strong in a world that wants you to crawl.*

"I'd say we have more than a little problem."

"Look, the briefcase is all yours, pal. Once Milton gets his daughter back, of course, and once the other hostages are handed over to me. Safe and sound. That's the deal. Take it or leave it."

Vic Gabriel stood in the corner of an empty apartment room. He was flanked by two Arabs with 5.45mm PSM pistols. The Soviet *Pistolet Samozaryadniy Malogabaritniy*, Gabriel recalled from his study of Eastern Bloc armaments, resembled the Walther PP. Fixed-barrel blowback, double-action lock, firing a 5.45×18mm bottle-neck-shaped cartridge of low power, but with enough velocity to get the job done. For concealment purposes, the Soviet PSM couldn't be beaten.

The Arab who had introduced himself as Hamil el Bejin had a Czech M61 Skorpion submachine pistol strapped around his shoulder. Bejin also had Gabriel's Detonics .45 tucked inside his black sash. Milton's briefcase rested on top of a small wooden table in the middle of the room. The briefcase was the "little problem" in question. It was more than just that to Gabriel. His life was on the line.

Bejin stepped up to Gabriel. A strange smile twisted the Arab's lips. Suddenly the smile vanished.

"And if I say, leave it, your deal?"

Gabriel said nothing.

"You understand, then, that you are in no position to dictate terms."

"Let's get on with it, Bejin. You get your money when the hostages are handed over. How much more simply can I put it?"

"Not so fast. Things here are not as simple as you would have me believe. You see, I have had some experience with your country's CIA in the past. Gabriel, you said your name was?"

"Just like the angel."

Bejin clasped his hands behind his back, began pacing back and forth in front of Gabriel. "Well, Gabriel, you look like CIA to me. I don't like CIA. I have killed CIA agents before. Slowly, and in great pain. This whole *deal* of yours would appear to be a setup."

"*Would* appear, yeah. It isn't. Look, Bejin, I'm only doing as I'm instructed by Milton. I'm nothing more than a delivery boy. You want to open that briefcase, be my guest. But can you do it after I've left the room?"

With cold eyes, Bejin looked at Gabriel. "You are going nowhere except with us. The briefcase will come. You will come. We have a little ride ahead of us, Gabriel. If, as I now suspect, you've been followed, you will be the first to die. Am I making myself perfectly clear?"

Gabriel drew a deep breath, exhaled. The testing grounds for Eagle Force had arrived.

Ground Zero.

He only hoped Zac Dillinger's P.I. skills hadn't grown rusty during the past few days. If Dillinger, Simms, and Boolewarke couldn't dog these fanatics to wherever he was being taken . . .

Vic Gabriel had more than just a little problem, right. But, for some reason, he felt right at home in the midst of a bubbling cauldron of potential violence.

He was back. Back in hell.

The Eye of the Fire waited.
Vic Gabriel burned inside, eager for action.


If it was obvious they were keeping the apartment complex under surveillance, Zac Dillinger didn't give a damn. Minutes ago, the P.I. had seen the Arab march Vic Gabriel into the building at gunpoint, and Dillinger was worried about his friend's neck. There was only one thing Dillinger hated worse than waiting for action to explode, and that was hearing, "The check's in the mail," from clients.

The narrow avenue was a beehive of activity, but Dillinger kept hard attention focused on the apartment building. He was sweating beneath the Arab robes and headcloth, and he was miserable as hell. The only cure for his discomfort, he knew, would be a firefight with the Sword of Islam. Johnny Simms and the Dutchman were directly across from Dillinger, the black merc and the ex-Recces commando standing watch in the mouth of the *suq*. Dillinger noticed the street people giving the three of them a mean eyeballing. But the scowl on the ugly face of the white-haired man could have cracked cement, and no one bothered the two Americans and the Dutchman.

"Did you see that?"

Dillinger looked at Simms. "See what?"

"To your left. One building down, four windows up. Try not to make it obvious when you look. 'Cause someone's watching us, Bad One."

Dillinger scoured the street, his gaze raking over the milling crowd. Squinting, he looked up. Sure enough, he saw two men in the window of the apartment building. There was a pair of binos in the hands of one man. The other guy stood behind his comrade.

"They're American, I'd bet my sister's ass in a whorehouse," Dillinger said.

"I didn't know you had a sister," Simms said.

"I don't."

"CIA, you think?" Simms posed.

"Well, there's only one way to find out," Dillinger said.

"You're not going in after them, are you?" Boolewarke asked.

"Have to," Dillinger said. "If we're being targeted by the CIA, I don't need to be looking over my shoulder for any more trouble than we've already got."

Boolewarke rasped out a breath. "We're only three. There's no telling if they have backup. The room could be packed with agents, if they're CIA."

"*If.* Hell, Dutch, one glance at those two and I can tell ya right now they're not girl watching. All right, so let's do this," Dillinger suggested. "Get the Land Rover, Johnny. Give us your map and me and the Dutchman will circle around and move in on those clowns." Dillinger caught Boolewarke's frown. "Two, three, ten, I don't care how many there are. Just keep Little Lightning ready."

"A firefight could blow the whole deal, hardhead," Boolewarke growled.

"You got a better suggestion?" Simms wanted to know.

Through the babble of conversation and the shouts of vendors in his ears, Dillinger heard Boolewarke curse. The Dutchman admitted that he wished he had a better idea.

Henry van Boolewarke thought that Zac Dillinger was a crazy bastard, reckless in his pursuit of danger, unmindful, it seemed, to the immediate threat to Vic Gabriel. The white-haired man's methods were certainly unorthodox. Dillinger, Boolewarke thought, would make a bull in a china shop look graceful. And, *ja*, Boolewarke doubted that Dillinger had any discipline at all when it came to executing an attack strategy. Mentally, Boolewarke had been sizing up Dillinger and Simms since he'd first laid eyes on them. The Dutchman didn't think either man would have lasted the selection course for the Recce commandos, which candidates had to endure for forty-two weeks in Zululand. Even if both men passed the Recce physical regimen, Boolewarke doubted they'd pass the psychological test. How Dillinger would fare in battle, Boolewarke was anxious to find out. Simms would have to wait in the wings for Boolewarke's judgment. Regardless of how Boolewarke knew Simms felt about him, the Dutchman would be every bit as harsh in his final analysis of Dillinger as he would be with the black American.

Dillinger checked the narrow hallway. They were alone. Mini-Uzi in his right hand, the Ka-Bar in his left, the white-haired man looked at Boolewarke, nodded. Helltime.

Fisting his own mini-Uzi, Boolewarke drew a Ka-Bar from the sheath inside his robe. Lifting his right leg, Boolewarke caved the door in with a thunderous kick. Flimsy wood shattered as the Dutchman hit a combat crouch.

"Freeze!" Dillinger boomed at the two men by the window.

Sprenger clawed for his shoulder-holstered .357 Colt Python Magnum. The CIA operative instantly regretted his impulse to react to danger.

"Asshole!" Dillinger hissed, and hurled his Ka-Bar.

Whirling through the air, the commando dagger speared into Sprenger's upper arm.

Swiftly, Dillinger, Little Lightning trained on Sprenger as the op crumpled to the floor, moved across the room. Running, Boolewarke was right on Dillinger's heels when Torquemada whipped a stainless steel .44 AutoMag from his shoulder holster. With a front snapkick, Boolewarke buried his boot into the op's gut. The AutoMag clattering to the stone floor, Torquemada crashed into the wall, face twisted in pain, his mouth vented as the air belched from his lungs. Still, Torquemada scrabbled across the floor, desperately reaching for the AutoMag.

Boolewarke kicked the op in the stomach with such

force that Torquemada snapped back into the wall like a rubber band.

"Mighty stupid thing to do, junior," the Dutchman rasped. "I could have kicked you in the face and killed you."

Dillinger pulled the dagger out of Sprenger's arm, picked up the Colt Python and tucked it inside his sash. "I'll tell ya what, Dutch," the P.I. said, as Boolewarke raked in the AutoMag. "I had my doubts about you, but I gotta admit—I kinda like your style."

Boolewarke didn't want the white-haired man's praise. Dillinger hadn't proven a damn thing yet, as far as the Dutchman was concerned. Boolewarke said nothing. Sometimes, he thought, it was best to let sleeping bullshitters dream.

Quickly, their mini-Uzis nearly stuck in the faces of the operatives, Boolewarke and Dillinger frisked Sprenger and Torquemada.

"Clean. No ID here. How about yours?" Dillinger asked.

"The same. No ID either. But they look dirty to me nonetheless."

Dillinger wiped the blood off his Ka-Bar on Sprenger's pantleg, sheathed the dagger. "Okay, boys, it's time to talk. Who are you? Who are you working for? And just what the fuck you watchin' us for?"

Torquemada showed Dillinger a bitter smile. "Go to hell."

"I was afraid you were going to say something like that." Dillinger shed his robe and *kaffiyah*. "What do you think, Dutch? Tie 'em up, then work on them?"

"We don't have the time. Gabe could be in trouble."

"Yeah, I suppose you're right, but I'm dying to get out of these damn things anyway. All right," he growled at the ops, "strip."

Sprenger and Torquemada looked at each other, angry, confused.

"I said, strip! You've got three seconds or I'll air-condition ya with Little Lightning here."

Moments later, both ops were stark naked. Ordering them to lie down on the floor and press their lips to stone, Dillinger and Boolewarke began cutting their robes into strips with the Ka-Bars.

"Since you're not going to cooperate," Dillinger said, "you leave us no choice but to let the maid find you in your birthday suits. We've got business to attend to, but I'm sure you already know that."

When he'd bound his captive's hands and feet, Boolewarke fisted a handful of Torquemada's hair. Yanking the operative's head up, he said, "Milton."

Torquemada was silent. But Boolewarke saw the man's gaze narrow a fraction of an inch.

"They know Milton," Boolewarke told Dillinger.

"How do you know that? What? Does that joker have lyin' eyes or somethin'?"

"Exactly."

"You learn something every day," Dillinger commented. Then he stuffed his *kaffiyah* into Sprenger's mouth. "You still think this was pointless, Dutch?"

Boolewarke said, "A little recklessness pays off once in a while . . . even for bulls."

"What's that supposed to mean?"

Boots pounded in the hallway.

Mini-Uzis in hand, Dillinger and Boolewarke whirled at the same instant.

Johnny Simms burst into the doorway. "They just left."

"Cold cock 'em, Dutch. Time to fly."

A right cross from Dillinger and Boolewarke hammered the ops into unconsciousness.

"The closet," Dillinger said, dragging Sprenger by the arm across the floor.

"Let's go! Let's go!" Simms urged. "We'll lose 'em."

"Relax, Johnny-Boy," Dillinger said, stuffing Sprenger into the closet. "We've got that homer, remember?"

Henry van Boolewarke tossed Torquemada on top of Sprenger. Glancing at Dillinger with hard eyes, holstering Little Lightning, Boolewarke took long strides across the room.

"What's the matter with you, Dutch?" Dillinger called out.

*Reckless and crazy and undisciplined*, Boolewarke thought about Dillinger and Simms. *Maybe . . . hell, just maybe they'll make it*.

# Chapter 10

With no idea where the fanatics were taking him, Vic Gabriel was searching for an answer to his present dilemma. Under guard in the back of a GAZ-66 Russian transport truck, Gabriel looked at the four Arabs sitting on the bench across from him. AK-47s resting between their legs, none of them would hesitate to put a 7.62mm ComBloc asshole between his eyes if Bejin gave them the order. For almost three hours, the Arabs had sat in cold silence, and Gabriel could sense the raw hatred they felt toward him, burning off their fatigues like the heat from a furnace. Russian arms. Russian truck. Gabriel wasn't surprised in the least by the material presence of Ivan. It was no secret that the Soviets supplied, armed, even outfitted major terrorist organizations. Détente was crap. Unfortunately, in their fear of Little Mother Russia, Gabriel thought, most of the West would believe what the Soviets told them, as long as the status quo was kept. Safeguarding the status quo meant doing anything, saying anything, believing anything to keep Ivan's fingers from pushing buttons. But the Russians, Gabriel firmly believed, weren't interested in committing suicide, either. It was the fanatic terrorist groups, like the Sword of Islam, that worried Gabriel. If by some chance they were to get their hands on nuclear firepower . . . Well, Iran had already tried that, and the Israelis had blown their plans back into the Stone Age.

Like most terrorists, the Sword of Islam fanatics came from poverty. The Soviets were masters at fomenting unrest, using a man's discontent, his envy of those who were well-off, and turning him into an instrument of terror and death and destruction. War-shattered Beirut was a natural breeding ground for Soviet cannon fodder. They might not realize it or, rather, care to admit it, Gabriel thought, but the Sword of Islam fanatics were merely Russian puppets. Promise them money. Promise them power and prestige. Whatever. When Russian puppets started taking innocent human life, Vic Gabriel believed it was time to cut the lifeline to the Hydra. With whatever it took. In the case of the *Sadi* fanatics, there was only one thing they understood, feared, and respected. A more savage force. A greater brute strength quite capable of trampling their flesh and bones into the dust.

Arms folded over his chest, Gabriel decided there was nothing he could do at the moment but feel the jar of the rough ride as the GAZ-66 bounded on toward its destination. Four times, the truck had stopped. Each time, an Arab had hopped out of the bed. Checkpoints, Gabriel knew. Bejin wasn't bluffing about finding out if the Sword of Islam delegation was being followed. It was sheer oversight on the part of the Arabs that they hadn't found the mini-homing device on Gabriel. Before embarking for his meet with the Arabs in Carthage, Gabriel had placed the device, which had a maximum range of ninety kilometers, in a small pocket sewn to the back-inside of his right thigh. Gabriel could only hope that Simms, Dillinger, and Boolewarke weren't far behind. He had a good idea how the commandos of Eagle Force would tackle the situation. Knowing the three shock troopers as Gabriel did, he suspected they would roar straight ahead, guns blazing, and death be damned. Shock tactics were just fine with Gabriel. Shock tactics caught the enemy off guard. Shock tactics could throw the enemy into a panic. Unless the Arabs bound his hands, Gabriel would be free to start maiming and kicking ass when his troops blitzkrieged onto the scene. *If*—if they didn't meet fierce *Sadi* resistance in an ambush somewhere back up the road. Or perhaps, Gabriel thought, the checkpoints were there merely to alert Bejin that he was being followed. Then the fanatics could follow Eagle Force and seal a ring of fire on them from behind.

Suddenly, the transport truck shuddered to a halt. Doors opened and slammed. The trap was thrown back, and Bejin stood in the opening, flanked by three Arab gunmen.

"Out!" Bejin barked.

*This is it*. Slowly, Gabriel stood. Weapons trained on him, Gabriel hopped out of the bed on the heels of his Arab guards. Right away, Gabriel checked his surroundings. And once again he felt as if he'd stepped back in time by about two thousand years. He looked at the crumbled ruins of the coliseum.

"You have arrived at El Djem. Do you recognize the Roman Thysdrus?" Bejin asked.

"Can't say I do."

"It is sad," Bejin said, gazing at the Roman Thysdrus.

"What's that?" Gabriel asked, not really giving a damn, but figuring Bejin was leading up to some revelation.

"The coliseum would be immaculate, but the locals here looted it for stone for their homes. And still, the Tunisians here in El Djem live like dogs in their hovels of stone and straw."

Gabriel looked at the massive stone coliseum. The sky hung, crimson, over the site where, Gabriel was certain, thousands had gone to their deaths for the amusement of the Romans. How many combatants had hacked each other to death in that charnel house? How many men and women had been ripped apart by lions in that arena of slaughter?

Except for the coliseum, the city of El Djem appeared unimpressive to Gabriel. Walled one-story houses stretched away from the coliseum. El Djem seemed deserted, except for a group of half-naked children playing in the distance. With the tightly packed rows of dirty-looking houses that seemed to reach like one endless lump away from the coliseum, the immediate vicinity looked wretched, and the air smelled of sweat, rot, and garbage. Before he was shoved toward the coliseum, Gabriel spotted a beaten-up Peugeot turning, then vanishing behind an eyesore of *ghourbis*, one-room shacks of stick and mud.

"Now we wait."

Gabriel detected the suspicion in Bejin's voice. "For what?"

"For . . . whatever . . . or whoever."

Gabriel was led between two massive pillars. Gut instinct warned Gabriel that his commandos were going to be welcomed at the coliseum by an ambush.

"How many do you think have died here, Gabriel?"

"What would you think if I said, not enough?"

Four Arabs, AK-47s in their hands, walked out of the shadows of the maw to the coliseum. Gabriel could smell the decay in the air. He could smell death.

Bejin was still looking at Gabriel, as if he was chewing over in his mind the ex-assassin's last words.

Recon was over.

Three shadows crouched beside the walled house.

Eagle Force, togged in combat black, was armed to the teeth.

The coliseum loomed before Simms, Dillinger, and Boolewarke, a dark, imposing stone mastodon bathed in the shadows of twilight. Probing the perimeter of the coliseum less than thirty minutes ago, the commandos had discovered the ancient slaughterground was enemy turf.

"Roman Thysdrus," Boolewarke muttered.

"You mean this is some arena where the Christians were fed to the lions?" Simms asked, the M16 in his hands, the M203 grenade launcher loaded with a 40mm hellbomb.

Boolewarke, the MM-1 multiround projectile launcher

117

strapped around his shoulder, loaded an arrow in the Barnett Panzer crossbow. "Christians, Berbers, it didn't matter to the Romans. Anything that could bleed was fine with them. If it moved, they'd want to see it hacked up. In some cases, they'd fuck it first, then hack it to pieces. Man, woman, child, lion. It was all the same. When you've reached the top like they did, there's only one place to go from there."

A mangy black mongrel trotted across the thirty-meter stretch of no-man's-land that separated the houses from the maw of the coliseum. There were no civilians in sight. It was as if the coliseum was a contaminated symbol of death, a grim reminder of an ugly past that no Tunisian in his right mind wanted to be near.

The HK G-11 ready for action, Dillinger scoured the columns along the rim of the coliseum. "Up there. I just spotted one."

Sure enough, as Simms and Boolewarke looked up, they saw the muzzle of an AK-47 assault rifle poking skyward.

"Bingo," Simms said, tight-lipped. "Showtime."

Dillinger took the receiver out of his pants pocket. "I know I already checked, but checking again's for my own peace of mind. Just in case they've moved him." The light flashed on the receiver. Turning the volume down, Dillinger listened to the soft hum. "Good. V.G.'s here, all right. Dumbasses didn't think to look between his legs for the homer."

"Didn't you know homosexuality is the one thing I hear the Muzzies frown upon?" Simms said.

"What's that got to do with anything?" Boolewarke gruffed.

"Well, if you didn't want to be thought of as a faggot by your bros, would you go stickin' your hands between a dude's legs and start feelin' around his plumbing?"

"You got a smart mouth," Boolewarke rasped.

"It keeps me runnin'."

The Dutchman's lips slitted into a sneer. "Toward or away from trouble?"

"To, stormtrooper. So, let's roll, huh?" Simms growled.

"We'll see how good you are," Boolewarke retorted.

"Hey, Dutch, Johnny-Boy, let's cut with the squabbling, huh. Christ, I didn't ride for damn near four hours in the cab of that Land Rover to come here and listen to a bitch session."

"By the pillars. He's mine. Get ready to move out," Boolewarke said.

An Arab sentry, his AK-47 canted to his shoulder, stepped away from the pillars.

Boolewarke drew target acquisition, triggered the crossbow. The broadhead arrowpoint drilled into the sentry's chest.

As Simms and Dillinger sprinted toward the wall of the coliseum, the sentry spun with the impact of the arrow. Unfortunately, Boolewarke discovered they were suddenly faced with disaster.

Autofire erupted, as the dying sentry squeezed off a short burst from his AK-47, then toppled.

"Shit!" Simms hissed, throwing himself up against the wall. "It ain't like the movies, is it, Bad One? They don't always die when they should."

Plucking MK2 frag grenades off their webbing, Dillinger and Simms slid down the wall.

Boolewarke unslung his MM1, expecting the worst.

The worst happened.

The columns along the rim of the coliseum blazed with muzzle flashes.

Combat senses on full alert, Simms and Dillinger pulled the pins on their grenades. An Arab whipped around the corner, his Kalashnikov chattering. But Dillinger dropped the Sword of Islam terrorist in his track with a three-round stutter from his G-11.

Slugs raking the ground before him, ComBloc lead

whining off the stone wall above him, Boolewarke triggered three rounds from the MM-1. Chugging from the MM-1, the trio of 38mm warheads streaked for the rim of the coliseum on a true line of destruction.

Reaching the edge of the wall, Dillinger and Simms lobbed the frag grenades around the corner. Explosions puked along the rim of the coliseum above the two commandos.

Between the pillars to the entrance, the frag grenades erupted in a gush of fire and flying steel fragments. Screams pierced the maw of the coliseum. Wheeling into the smoke, Simms and Dillinger opened up with their weapons, as rubble and shredded stick figures of men rained to no-man's-land. Weapons stammering, Dillinger and Simms scythed through a half-dozen Arab fanatics with a combined lead hellstorm of 5.56mm slugs and 4.7mm flesh-eaters.

Henry van Boolewarke charged toward the coliseum, the MM-1 belching 40mm warheads toward the rim of the Roman Thysdrus.

Bodies crunched to no-man's-land. Rubble pelted the earth behind Boolewarke.

# Chapter 11

Vic Gabriel saw the terrorists as cockroaches, as they scurried out of the smoke boiling between the pillars and surged across the arena. *Sadi*, once vultures preying on the innocent, now insects to be exterminated. Their crimes demanded their blood. And, yeah, Gabriel thought, *Sadi* had just met that more savage force. A juggernaut that was going to trample them into the dust. Eagle Force.

No more exchanges. No more haggling over the hostages. The fucking around, Gabriel thought, was over. And the ex-CIA assassin was primed to tear somebody's head off his shoulders.

Hamil el Bejin and another Arab were Gabriel's closest targets at the moment.

As autofire ripped across the arena and *Sadi* soldiers tumbled to the dirt, Gabriel leapt to his feet.

Bejin's Czech M61 swung toward Gabriel. There was a look of maniacal rage in Bejin's eyes. His expression was carved by agony a millisecond later, as the steel-tipped toe of Gabriel's commando boot shattered Bejin's wrist. Howling, the Skorpion submachine pistol flying from his hands, Bejin reeled, stumbled, slammed off the edge of the stone steps. It was a long tumble down those steps from the second tier, Bejin's arms flailing, his head cracking off stone.

Bejin down for the count, Gabriel turned grim death-sights on the Arab gunman to his left. Wheeling, Gabriel drove the heel of his boot into the Arab's kneecap. Stuttering, the AK-47 spat flame, and Gabriel felt the hot lead whiz past his face. Following up on the kick, Gabriel pulped the Arab's nose to crimson mush with the heel of his palm, strangling the terrorist's scream as his nosebone was driven into his brain. Before the Arab hammered to the steps, Gabriel ripped the AK-47 out of his hands.

And not a second too soon.

Three Arabs, huddled in the entranceway that led to dungeons below the arena, where gladiators had been incarcerated alongside the lions in the days of Roman-occupied North Africa, kept Simms, Dillinger, and Boolewarke pinned down behind the pillars with relentless autofire. Gabriel started running down the steps, angling for a clear shot at the enemy; stone chips suddenly spat up at his heels. Spotting the face of fear below him, Gabriel triggered his Kalashnikov.

A tracking line of deadly accurate autofire shattered the face of fear into a death mask.

Intent on blowing the Arabs in the dungeon entranceway into eternity himself, Gabriel saw Johnny Simms trigger his M203. Muzzling at seventy-one meters per second, the 40mm grenade impacted in the heart of the three fanatics. Shredded meat, bits and pieces of those terrorists plastered the walls of the dungeon entrance, a greasy scarlet stain. Smoke drifted out of the dungeon's maw. A bloodstained headcloth floated to the arena.

Less than two eyeblinks later, the battle ended.

Combined autofire from Simms and Dillinger crucified six fleeing Arabs to the wall of the first tier. Chunks of bloody cloth sheared off their chests, the Arabs twisted, slid down the wall.

Securing cover behind the wall in front of the first tier, four fanatics raked the position of the commandos with a 7.62mm typhoon. Dropping to his right knee, Boolewarke triggered two 38mm warheads from the MM-1. The double explosion meshed, hurling the Arabs up the steps on a boiling cloud of fire.

Grim-faced, moving into the arena, Gabriel surveyed the carnage.

A groan.

The dead came to life.

Two *Sadi* fanatics clawed for their Russian assault rifles. Outstretched on his stomach, just yards away from the three commandos of Eagle Force, one of the two Arabs hauled in an AK-47, wobbled to his feet. Then, like a scarecrow in a hurricane, that Arab was kicked back by a gale-force pounding of 5.56mm slugs flaming from the muzzle of Johnny Simms's M16.

The magazine in his HK G-11 expended, Dillinger strode into the arena. Unleathering one of his Colt .45s, the white-haired commando pumped a slug into the face of the other Arab as the terrorist rolled onto his back. Twitching, the dead terrorist squeezed off a short burst from his AK-47, then lay utterly still.

The Kalashnikov low by his side, Gabriel stepped toward the motionless figure of Bejin. "I could've used a hostage, Zac. How do you think we're going to find the rest of these shitsuckers?"

Dillinger grunted. "Got a little trigger happy, V.G. My mistake. I'll file away what you just said for future reference."

"Do that." Gabriel couldn't find Johnny Simms. "Where's Simms?"

"Johnny-Boy's covering the front," Dillinger answered, holstering his Blood and Guts special and scouring the tiers. Then he searched the crumbled ruins of vaulted galleries along the rim of the coliseum for any sign of enemies in hiding. Nothing but the dead.

Real pros, Gabriel thought about Simms, Dillinger, and Boolewarke. If he'd had any doubts before about the three commandos pulling together as a team in a firefight, the slaughter around Gabriel was evidence enough that he'd chosen the right men. He was reminded of something his father once told him in Special Forces.

*"It's important to be an individual, son. A man has to stand on his own two feet, make tough decisions. There comes a time, though, when that individual has to be a team player. When on an SFG operation, your primary allegiance is to your detachment. 'Heroes' get men killed or injured, and everything I've taught you won't be worth a damn if you get yourself, or worse, one of your own, killed."*

Individuals pulling together as a team in the Eye of the Fire. That was what Gabriel had just witnessed. He was proud of Simms, Dillinger, and Boolewarke. Whether or not that spirit would last . . .

"Was that all of the bastards?" Boolewarke called out to Gabriel, the Dutchman reloading the empty chambers of the MM-1.

"I don't know, Dutch, I didn't take a headcloth count," Gabriel answered. "Keep your eyes peeled anyway. Some snake may slither out of a hole. Let me ask you, were you followed here?"

"I don't know," Dillinger answered. "I don't think so. I hope not."

"Well, which is it?" Gabriel growled.

"We didn't see anybody. Why?" Dillinger asked.

"Because they dropped off shitsuckers along the way, that's why," Gabriel answered. "We've got enough trouble ahead of us without having to be looking over our shoulders from here on out."

"I hear ya. Speaking of trouble, I suggest we get the hell outta here, Vic," Dillinger said. "Before whatever pass for local cops surround this place."

Gabriel agreed. First, though, he wanted to retrieve his Detonics .45 from Bejin. Damn, but he would've liked to have bagged a prisoner. Damn, but . . .

Suddenly, Gabriel saw Bejin stir. Draped over the

edge of a step, blood poured out of the Arab's mouth. Cuts and bruises masked Bejin's face.

Gabriel bent over Bejin, plucked the Detonics .45 out of the Arab's sash. Snatching a handful of Bejin's hair, Gabriel shook Bejin's head. "Wake up, Abdul. Wake up! I don't have time for dicking around," he growled.

Bejin pried his eyelids open. "I think my back's . . . broken."

"For your sake," Gabriel rasped, "you'd better hope it is."

With no time to waste on Bejin, Gabriel determined there was only one way to find out how badly the Arab terrorist was injured. Gabriel grabbed Bejin by the shirt-front and hauled the Arab to his feet. Clutching his broken wrist, Bejin cried out.

"Where's the briefcase, Abdul?"

Bejin looked at Gabriel with defiant hatred. Finally, he said, "In the truck. Beneath the seat."

"All that cash, and you leave it lying around for anybody to pick up?"

Bejin showed Gabriel a twisted smile. "I thought it was rigged to blow up if opened. Unless you lied?"

"I just didn't tell you the whole truth, Abdul. The money's not real."

"Wh-what?"

Gabriel jabbed Bejin in the back with the muzzle of his AK-47. "Move it, Abdul. You're going home. You've got an appointment."

*Sadi* had already paved their own path into hell. The only thing left to do was seal the lid on their tomb and let the bastards burn. But that was something, Gabriel suspected, easier said than done.

Much easier.

Gabriel slung Bejin to the ground. Simms killed the Land Rover's engine but left the lights on, bathing Bejin in a blinding white curtain. Bejin squinted into the light. Gabriel stomped on Bejin's broken wrist.

"Aaaaaahhhh!!!"

The cry of torment echoed off into the darkness.

Gabriel removed his foot from Bejin's wrist. Almost two hours north of El Djem, Gabriel had long since lost his patience with Bejin. Hard questioning and ugly threats had gotten Gabriel nowhere with his prisoner. It was time to play hardball. "North" had been Bejin's only answer when Gabriel asked the terrorist where the Sword of Islam fanatics were holed up.

Filing out of the Land Rover, the three commandos of Eagle Force stood just outside the light, dark, silent shadows.

"What are you protecting, Abdul?" Gabriel began again, for the fourth time. The same questions, but not the same tactics anymore. If Bejin didn't wise up, interrogation would become execution. "Your brothers in the holy war? You think you're protecting them? You think you can hold out here in Tunisia forever? Well, let me tell you something, Abdul, four Grim Reapers have come to Tunisia to spill some blood. Lots of blood. *Sadi* blood. You've already seen we're not fucking around."

With defiant hatred, Bejin looked up at Gabriel. Bejin spat.

Suddenly, Gabriel drew his Detonics .45, cannoned a round that drilled into the earth beside Bejin's head. Bejin flinched. Gabriel kicked Bejin in the balls. Grunting, trying to stifle a scream, the Arab doubled-up into a fetal position. Hands clutching at his punished manhood, Bejin cursed.

"I bet that felt good," Dillinger dryly commented.

With a Zippo, Simms fired up a cigarette. "Be a whole lot easier, Abdul, if you cooperated with the man."

"Why should I?" Bejin hissed. "He's going to kill me anyway."

"Maybe . . . maybe not," Gabriel told the terrorist. "You tell us where your brothers in murder are hiding out, take us there, I'll make a decision. No promises, though. And no crap from you."

Bejin laughed. "I am looking at four men. I saw four men get lucky back at El Djem. Do you think you would be so lucky against a force of forty?"

"Ten-to-one odds," Boolewarke mused. "I always did like a challenge."

"You're fools," Bejin snarled.

Gabriel aimed the Detonics at Bejin's face. "You've got three seconds. One . . . two . . ."

"All right, I'll take you there!"

"Where?"

"Northwest of Tunis. In the Atlas Mountains."

"You're talking about another hundred-plus miles," Dillinger said to Gabriel.

"We've got three drums of fuel in the bed of the Land Rover," Gabriel reminded him. "But I wonder if Adbul might not be leading us into an ambush. How about it, Adbul? You dropped a few of your people off on the way to El Djem."

Groaning, Bejin rolled up on his side. "They were merely lookouts. They were supposed to have contacted me by radio if they saw anything suspicious. Unfortunately, our radio broke down just after we arrived at El Djem. Now, do you see what I mean by luck? Had we known that three of your killers were coming, we would have been ready, and they would have died.

"As for the ambush, I have no intention of leading you into a trap. You see, you think I do this to save my own life. But I do this to see you dead, because you are only four against forty. And I do it for her."

Gabriel's gaze narrowed. "Her?"

Bejin smiled triumphantly. "Yes, her. Pamela Milton We're lovers."

Simms whistled. "Man, that's gonna break the old man's heart."

Gabriel nodded. *So much for her inheritance,* he wryly thought. *What a slap in the old man's face this will be.*

"So why tell me this?" Gabriel wanted to know.

"It is easy enough to understand. You are enemies of Islam. You were sent by her father to rescue her—big American heroes."

"So, it makes Abdul there," Dillinger said, "feel good to throw some shit in the old man's face. Makes sense in a twisted kind of way. But if we're going to die, like you claim, how are you going to be able to smear shit on the old man's face?"

"You will have done it for me in death," Bejin answered. "He will know you have failed. The hostages will be executed. All of them, except his daughter. She will then tell him the truth. He will then know he sent you on a fool's errand."

"And I'm feelin' more foolish by the hour," Simms said. "And just a little worried."

"You haven't forgotten the men we found in the apartment in Tunis, have you, Vic?" Boolewarke asked. "I they are CIA . . ."

"No, I haven't forgotten, Dutch. Just more trouble. My feeling is they came alone or you would've run into their backup on the way out. They should stay put until we can get back to Milton."

"Get back," Bejin scoffed. "You're never going back, American hero."

"This guy's starting to bug me, Vic," Dillinger growled. "Why don't you just pump a round in his face, and let's get on with it."

Gabriel didn't exactly feel like dragging Bejin along for the ride, either, but Bejin knew where the *Sadi* compound was located, and that was the bottom line. If Bejin was lying, if the Arab led them into an ambush, Gabriel wouldn't hesitate to kill him—quickly, one bullet through the brain. After all, the *Sadi* bastard would do the same to him. An eye for an eye might make everybody blind, he thought, but this was a war of no compromise. Any less effort, and Vic Gabriel wouldn't have to worry about tomorrow.

Vic Gabriel hauled Bejin to his feet.

# Chapter 12

"Something is very wrong, Dhourjan. I can feel it in the air."

"What? What is it you feel, Muhmad?"

"Death."

Muhmad Hammadi was worried. Hamil el Bejin and the others should have returned from El Djem hours ago. At the least, someone should have radioed word to the compound. Either the ransom money had not been delivered, or . . . or what? Hammadi wondered. What could have gone wrong? Were they dead? Had they been captured by an enemy unwilling to fold and give in to his demands. If that had happened, what would he do? Hammadi asked himself. What *could* he do? Kill the hostages and send their mutilated bodies back to the United States? Kill Pamela Milton out of spite? No, he couldn't very well do that, Hammadi knew. If he did, there would certainly be no money, and without money, there would be no more weapons. Without cash, he couldn't hire and train more soldiers for the holy war, either. Muhmad Hammadi had never expected his task to be an easy one. Then again, he'd never expected resistance. If he was faced with a determined enemy ready to crush him . . . Well, he would just have to fight, to the death, if necessary. Yes, if he died in battle against an infidel force he would at least go to paradise. *Allah akbar*.

Standing beside the seven GAZ-66 transport trucks,

Hammadi scratched his beard, glanced up at a black velvet sky glittering with starlight. Silently, he prayed to Allah that his men were safe and that his plans would be fulfilled. It was such a calm, peaceful night, Hammadi thought. It would be tragic if something happened to spoil his plans. Peace, though, was not in Hammadi's heart. He felt like a caged animal. And as the minutes dragged by and there was still no word from Bejin, he was beginning to feel like a cornered animal, as well.

"It is, indeed, strange that no one has sent word," the short, stocky Dhourjan said, an AK-47 strapped around his shoulder.

"It is worse than that. I suspect Milton has planned to trick us, Dhourjan. Or worse, have us hit."

Dhourjan was shocked. "Our sentries have seen nothing, Muhmad. Surely . . ."

"Surely, what?" Hammadi rasped, then looked at Dhourjan, who appeared offended by his leader's brusque tone. "Look at these hills, Dhourjan. We are at the foothills of the Atlas Mountains. Forests cover these hills and mountains. Many trails lead up the back of the hills and down into the valley. Under the cover of night, a squad of assassins could move in on the compound and attack us. Unless Hamil returns with his men, we do not have enough soldiers to cover the entire perimeter of the compound and stand guard in the hills. I want the guard doubled around the hostages. Place two two-man fireteams in the hills to the north. Arm them with RPGs."

Moving away from the transport trucks, Dhourjan right on his heels, Hammadi cursed. He was suddenly very worried. Sick with worry.

"Where is she?" Hammadi asked Dhourjan.

"I am right here."

Hammadi stopped. Turning, he found a shadow standing near the GAZ-66 transport trucks. The voice and the well-rounded curves of the long, shapely figure betrayed the presence of Pamela Milton.

131

"How long have you been standing there?" Hammadi demanded to know.

"Long enough to know that we might be in trouble. Why has there been no word from Hamil?"

"You are not to worry about Hamil, do you understand? I am sure Hamil is fine and there is good reason why I have not heard from him."

"So you say."

Hammadi didn't like the woman's insolent tone. He took several steps toward Pamela Milton. Enough. He wanted to backhand the Western slut to the ground, then take her body right there. On her back, with her face in the dirt, better still. She had been nothing but trouble from the start, but Hamil had been blinded by his passions. It didn't matter to Hammadi anymore whether or not the woman believed in the *jihad*. Any fool could see that she was merely infatuated with the idea of revolution. She had told Hammadi more than once of her hatred for her father. Pamela Milton was merely an undisciplined, spoiled little rich bitch who was looking to get back at her father any way she could.

Perhaps the bitch was in love with Hamil after all. But if she really cared about Hamil el Bejin, why would she be so unfaithful to him? As soon as Hamil was out of sight, Hammadi could always expect Pamela Milton to come running to him. An Arab woman of loose morals would be shamed publicly by her husband and cast out to fend for herself. Perhaps, Hammadi thought, the woman was hungry for power, seeking to play both ends against the middle and set Hamil against him.

Thrusting his hands on his hips, Hammadi stared at the woman for a moment. He felt his temper ready to explode. He hated her, but he wanted her at the same time. If it weren't for his holy war, perhaps things would have been better between the two of them. She was fiery, impulsive, a sexual tigress. She spoke her mind, and she would let anyone, man or woman, know how she felt about anything, no matter what the consequences of her words. As much as he wanted to beat her to a pulp at that moment, Hammadi realized it would be a waste of energy.

"I will be perfectly honest with you," Hammadi began. "We have not heard from Hamil or the others. I do not know what has happened to them. I believe your father has double-crossed us. Now you tell me. Is it possible your father would hire mercenaries to come here and attempt a rescue?"

Pamela Milton shrugged. "I don't know. I really didn't know anything about my father's business. I hardly ever saw him when I was growing up, and I saw him even less these past few years since he divorced my mother."

Shutting his eyes, feeling a terrible weariness settle over him, Hammadi shook his head. "I don't want to hear about your bitterness and your family problems. I asked you a question."

"And I said, I don't know. What more can I tell you? With the money my father has, I suppose anything's possible."

"Yes," Hammadi agreed. "I suppose it is."

"Do you think we're going to be attacked?"

Hammadi looked hard at the woman, unable to believe the edge of excitement in her voice. The bitch actually wanted to fight an unknown enemy that might be coming after them. She was either brave or naive, he decided.

"And if we are? What will you do?" Hammadi asked.

"I will fight, of course. To the death, if necessary."

Hammadi wanted to laugh at her. *To the death*. She was naive. This woman who came from wealth and luxury knew nothing of death, he thought, and probably knew even less about suffering. Perhaps, Hammadi decided, it would be best if they were attacked and she was killed during the battle. At the least, it would prove interesting.

"Then," Hammadi told her, "you shall fight. To the death, if necessary."

Swiftly, silently, Eagle Force glided through the forest. Armed shadows, they moved under the cover of darkness.

The muzzle of his Detonics .45 pressed against the nape of Bejin's neck, Gabriel urged the Arab terrorist up the incline. Just over an hour ago, they'd left the Land Rover behind to begin the final leg toward their appointment with death. According to Bejin, the *Sadi* compound was located in a valley. The ridge that overlooked the valley was now in Gabriel's sight, less than fifty meters ahead.

M16 with an attached M203 grenade launcher strapped around his shoulder, Gabriel checked his shock troops. They were armed with the same weapons they'd used to slaughter the *Sadi* terrorists at the Roman Thysdrus. Spread out in a skirmish line, Simms and Dillinger flanked Gabriel, with Boolewarke covering the rear. For the moment, Eagle Force was closing in for silent kills. Boolewarke toted his favored Panzer Barnett crossbow, while Simms and Dillinger closed down on the ridge with Ka-Bars poised to deliver death. Yeah, Gabriel had good reason to suspect sentries were posted around the perimeter of the compound, certain that Hammadi had received word about the massacre of his troops at El Djem. If the Sword of Islam wasn't ready to fight this time, Gabriel thought, that was their tough shit. *Because hell's going to get mighty crowded after tonight, bet your ass.*

Pamela Milton now presented another problem to Gabriel. A wild card in the picture, the woman was a definite liability and would, most likely, hinder Gabriel's plans, before and after the battle. Bejin had already warned Gabriel that his lover would fight like a wildcat when the battle began. Great. All Gabriel needed now was to have to kill Milton's daughter. Which presented another problem. Payment. Whether or not he, in fact, had to kill Pamela Milton, Gabriel knew the old man was going to get mean and ugly when he learned the truth about his daughter's involvement with the Sword of Islam. Gabriel wasn't looking forward to telling Milton about his daughter—hell, no. It wasn't that he was afraid of Milton and his bodyguards. Rather, he could just hear Milton refusing to pay them now. If any of Eagle Force survived the engagement with *Sadi* and an angry, vindictive Milton refused to deliver the rest of the money, it would just be lighting a fuse that would ignite the commandos.

And to make matters worse, the CIA was hunting him. Trouble, trouble, and more trouble. And the gates of hell were just opening.

Then Gabriel spotted the sentries standing guard before those gates. Two shadows with AK-47s stood along the ridge, one guard to the far left of Gabriel, the other one to his right. Stopping, Gabriel crouched behind a tree. He pulled Bejin down. With a wave of his hand, Gabriel gave Boolewarke and Dillinger the signal. Simms looked at Gabriel, but the ex-CIA assassin shook his head. Simms understood, stayed put. It was man-on-man time, and three was a crowd.

"You even breathe too loud," Gabriel whispered in Bejin's ear. "You'll have your lips around Satan's cock before you even hit the ground."

As silent as a ghost, Boolewarke moved past Gabriel. Dillinger, the Ka-Bar low by his side, blade angled up, closed down on the sentry to Gabriel's left.

Boolewarke hit a combat crouch. With the crossbow, he drew target acquisition, waited.

Gabriel saw Dillinger surge up on his target from behind. Dillinger clasped his right hand over the sentry's mouth. There was a brief struggle, then the sentry went limp in Dillinger's arms.

Boolewarke triggered the crossbow. Downrange, the Dutchman found his mark with deadly accuracy.

A soft thud, then a muffled cry. The arrow's shaft

jutting from his back, just to the left of his spine, Boole
warke's victim pitched into the brush.

Hustling Bejin to the ridge, Gabriel shoved the ter
rorist down.

"Looks clean this way, Victor," Johnny Simms tol
Gabriel.

"Nothing this way, either," Boolewarke answered from
Gabriel's left flank.

Holstering his Detonics .45, Gabriel unslung his M16
stretched out in a prone position beside Bejin. Comba
senses on full alert, Gabriel took in the compound and it
surroundings as Dillinger, Simms, and Boolewarke, cov
ered behind the dense brush, kept searching the ridge fo
any sign of more sentries. It was a big, deep valley, an
Gabriel knew the enemy could be hiding anywhere dow
the slopes that led to the compound. Boulders also studde
the hillside. Sixth sense warned Gabriel that the enemy wa
waiting.

The compound itself didn't look like much to Gabriel
Two long rows of barracks ran through the middle of th
compound. Barbed-wire ringed the *Sadi* base. A lone klie
light shed a white hue over the compound. To the nort
there was a mountainous pile of what looked like ashes.

"Where are the hostages being kept?" Gabriel aske
Bejin.

Bejin grunted, hesitated. Gabriel dug the muzzle o
his M16 into Bejin's ribs.

"I asked you a question."

"You would shoot me in cold blood right here and ris
alerting them?"

"Right."

"So be it. There. Beside the ammo depot."

Gabriel followed Bejin's dark stare. Six Arabs wit
AK-47s were clustered around a small wooden structure a
the far west edge of the base. The ammo depot, a large hu
made of tin, sat next to where the hostages were bein

guarded. Gabriel then spotted the Russian transport trucks to the south.

"What's in the trucks?"

"Fuel. For the trucks and the flamethrowers."

Gabriel heard Johnny Simms mutter an oath.

"Flamethrowers?" the black commando echoed.

"Human barbecue," Bad Zac Dillinger grimly commented.

"What are you talking about now?" Boolewarke gruffed from beside Dillinger.

"Skewering some fanatics and roasting their murdering asses, Dutch, that's what I'm talking about."

Right, Vic Gabriel thought. *Human barbecue.* Now that he was there, right on top of the fanatics and ready to deal out death, Gabriel suddenly replayed the vision of the Paris massacre through his mind. The human pyre in that cafe. Innocent victims whose lives had been snuffed out by the madness of evil ambition. It was payback time for the Sword of Islam. Long ago, *Sadi* had signed the contract for slaughter. Their own slaughter.

Glancing left then right, Gabriel nodded. Eagle Force knew what to do.

Silently, M16 in hand, Boolewarke fell in beside Johnny Simms. Seconds later, the Dutchman and the black commando vanished into the forest.

"All right, Zac," Gabriel said, turning and looking Dillinger dead in the eye.

"This is it, Vic, huh? Move in, wait until Johnny-Boy and Dutch draw their fire?"

"Just like we discussed. There's only one way to nail . . ."

Before Gabriel could react, Bejin was scrambling down the slope, shouting like a madman.

"Muhmad! Muhmad! We are being attacked! We are being . . ."

"Sonofabitch!" Dillinger rasped.

A three-round burst stammered from Gabriel's M16.

The line of 5.56mm slugs stitching up his spine, Bejin cried out. Nose-diving to the slope, Bejin tumbled down the hillside.

A second klieg light flared on.

"Let's move it, Zac! I think we just lost the element of surprise."

"Tell me about it, V.G."

Shadows charged from around the corners of the barracks.

The finger of blinding white light washed over the slopes below Gabriel. Without hesitation, Gabriel and Bad Zac Dillinger closed down the *Sadi* compound.

Vic Gabriel triggered his M16.

Helltime.

The war was on.

# Chapter 13

Not a second too soon, Gabriel shattered the klieg light with a three-round 5.56mm burst as the white glare swept toward him. The treeline giving way to hard barren earth, Gabriel and Dillinger crouched behind a boulder. Ahead of Gabriel and Dillinger stretched about twenty meters of no-man's-land that separated the hills from the barbed wire. It was going to be no easy task to get inside that compound, free the hostages, and exfiltrate. Most likely, they'd be retreating, with the Sword of Islam fanatics right on their heels, guns blazing in the name of Allah. Right. So be it. There was only one way to get into the compound and get out again: kill anything that moved in the name of Muhammad. It was time to run with the devil, Gabriel thought.

Gabriel saw the enemy scrambling into defensive positions behind the barbed wire. Two three-round bursts from the chattering M16s in the hands of Gabriel and Dillinger ventilated four headclothed Russian puppets. Blood jetting from stomachs bursting open and throats chewed up by the NATO lead sizzlers, those Arabs danced a jig of death, reeling into the barbed wire. There, they bobbed, crimson juices gushing from gaping holes in their chests, pearly-white strands of guts worming from their bullet-gutted breadbaskets and spilling to the ground.

Eight other Arabs bellyflopped to the ground behind the barbed wire, unleashing an AK-47 autostorm. As the typhoon of ComBloc lead ripped into the trees behind them and ricocheted off rock, Gabriel and Dillinger, stone chips stinging their faces, unloaded 40mm hellbombs from their M203s. Downrange, the double blast puked a huge ball of fire through the Arabs, hurling bodies and coiled strands of wire skyward. As shredded chunks of meat spattered the ground, Gabriel and Dillinger reloaded their M203s. Having now paved the way into the hellgrounds, Gabriel and Dillinger charged the compound.

*Death be damned!*

The strike zone, Gabriel knew, was wide open for a blitzkrieg hurricane.

Johnny Simms and Henry van Boolewarke could fend for themselves; Gabriel concentrated full, deadly attention on the immediate enemy targets. Purposely, Gabriel had thrown those two men together: the best way to overcome mutual animosity was in the heat of battle. Fear of death was stronger than personal feelings and slanted opinions.

Cordite and the smell of blood in his nose, Gabriel vaulted over the barbed wire.

Autofire blistered the night.

Gabriel hit the ground, rolled as a line of tracking fire hosed the earth behind him. Up and running, Gabriel glimpsed a shadow out of the corner of his eye. Switching the mode on his M16 to full-auto, Gabriel raked the corner of the barracks with a wild spray of lead. He heard the scream, knew he'd struck flesh. It was a lucky shot, Gabriel realized, as he saw the Arab spin away from the barracks and topple, AK-47 flying from his hands. Gabriel didn't mind taking a little luck, now and again.

"Vic! Look!"

Throwing himself against the corner of the barracks, Gabriel looked toward the ammo depot and the hut. He cursed.

Muhmad Hammadi stepped through the doorway of the hut. Four *Sadi* fanatics followed, each pressing the muzzle of an AK-47 against the side of a hostage's head.

"Shit," Dillinger rasped. "Don't fuckin' tell me . . . we got a standoff, Arab style."

Behind the far corners of the barracks, Arab gunmen crouched, AK-47s poised to fire.

"Not hardly," Gabriel said. "Get ready."

"For what?"

"Some fireworks. Then some sniping. Hold your fire, though, until I give you the word."

Gabriel heard Dillinger groan. Turning, he read the pain in Dillinger's eyes. Then he saw the blood pouring from the wound in the P.I.'s upper chest. The M16 slung around his shoulder, the P.I. brandished one of his Blood and Guts specials in his left hand.

"Passed clean through," Dillinger growled through gritted teeth. "I think the goddamn sonofabitchin' slug shattered my collarbone, though."

"I didn't even hear you cry out. I didn't even know."

"You weren't supposed to. I'm a tough guy, remember? Now, what's this about some fireworks?"


They were drawing target acquisition with the RPG-7s when two shadows swept up on the four Arabs from behind. M16s blazing, Dillinger and Boolewarke drove the rocket fireteams into each other with a fusillade of flesh-shredding 5.56mm slugs.

Simms scooped up an RPG-7, slung the rocket launcher around his shoulder. "Never can tell, I might be able to use one of these Ivan cannons. Whaddaya think, stormtrooper?"

"I just hope we didn't alert a small army," Boolewarke snarled, searching the forest around him. "That's what I think."

South, less than a hundred meters away from them, the battle raged, a furious din of autofire and explosions.

A sudden lull in the firefight saved the lives of Henry

van Boolewarke and Johnny Simms. Brush rattled, and Simms spotted the enemy.

"Behind you!" Simms hollered, the M16 swinging toward the shadow as flames erupted from the muzzle of an AK-47. On full-auto slaughter, Simms raked the trees and brush, emptying a dozen rounds into three Arabs, scything them down like wheat. Or was it four gunmen? Simms wondered, as bodies pirouetted and vanished from his sight. It was hard to tell the numbers in the darkness of the forest.

Simms saw Boolewarke backpedal, drop to the ground. The Dutchman's head cracked against a rock. Simms thought he spotted blood soaking down the pant leg of the Afrikaaner, but he couldn't be sure. Simms took a step toward Boolewarke.

Then the night suddenly came alive with fury.

A shadow bounded over the boulder beside Simms, rocketing toward the black commando.

"*Iswaaaahhh!*"

The Arab battle cry froze Simms in his tracks for a crucial heartbeat. Spotting the *jambiya* raised above the Arab's head to deliver a skull-shattering deathblow, Simms triggered his M16. Nothing. The magazine empty, Simms thrust the barrel up. Metal banged into the M16's barrel, jarring Simms to the bone. The weight of the Arab crashing into him, Simms toppled on his back, his head hammering the earth hard, stars exploding in his sight. There was a horrible rasping noise in Simms's ears. He smelled sweat. And blood. Feeling the blood spray over his face, Simms realized he'd drilled the Muslim bastard good before he'd spent his last 5.56mm slug in the thirty-round magazine. Or had he been hit? Simms wondered. Then he saw the agony etched into his attacker's face, knew the Arab fanatic was in great pain. But that gave the black commando little satisfaction as he realized he had a maniac prepared to fight to the death on his hands.

Whipping his leg up to drill the Muslim in the chest,

Simms say the dark shape loom up behind the knife-wielding devil.

Boolewarke curled his arm around the Muslim's shoulder, locking the Arab's knifehand before he could strike Simms.

Simms watched, but it was over in the blink of an eye. Death struck, lightning fast.

The Ka-Bar sliced across the Muslim's throat, cutting deep. Like a torn hose, blood jetted from the Arab's severed jugular veins. As if the Arab was nothing more than a sack of garbage, Boolewarke tossed the fanatic away.

For long moments, Boolewarke and Simms locked stares. Johnny Simms didn't know what to say to the man he thought of as a South African stormtrooper, a racist, part of a regime more racist than the American South up to the Civil War. Personal feelings aside, maybe the dude was all right. He thought about thanking the Dutchman, but he just couldn't bring himself around to it.

Boolewarke prodded his side where three slugs had ripped out flesh. Sheathing his blood-dripping blade, the Dutchman snatched up his M16.

"Let's move it! There's a war on," Boolewarke growled. "Johnny-Boy," he added, a thin smile ghosting his lips.

Simms stood, slapped home a fresh thirty-round clip into the M16's magazine. Maybe, Simms thought, it's false pride that keeps the whole human race living in fear of each other. The Dutchman had just saved his life. He didn't want to feel like he owed the Dutchman. He figured a simple thanks was in order.

"Hey, man!"

Boolewarke stopped near the edge of the treeline. Turning, he growled back at Simms, "Don't say it. You may regret it later. Besides . . . you just killed a couple more than I did, but who's keeping count?"

Muhmad Hammadi was keeping count—a body count. And the leader of the Sword of Islam figured his force had been ripped in half by the mystery attackers. It was time to seize the night. With brutal force. *The infidels must die!*

Using a hostage as a shield, his AK-47 jammed into the nape of his captive's neck, Hammadi spotted the heads of the two men poking around the corner at the end of the barracks. There was no way, he believed, feeling rage and confusion, that only two men could wreak such havoc on so many determined soldiers for the cause. It couldn't be possible.

And what had happened to his fireteams with the RPG-7s? Hammadi wondered. What were they waiting for? Why hadn't they blown the infidels off the face of Tunisia? Unless, he feared, those soldiers had already gone to paradise.

"You! You, there! Throw down your weapons and come out! I promise you, as Allah is my witness, that you will be treated honorably. If you do not surrender, I will kill all the hostages. Believe me, I will."

"He's not lying," one of the hostages called out. "He's already murdered one of us!"

"Silence!" Hammadi hissed at the hostage.

"We've got a problem here, Hammadi," Vic Gabriel called out. "It's called justice. You want us; we want a piece of you. We figure you for shit, and we're the justice that's going to sanitize you and that chickenshit puke you call warriors. So, why don't you just let the hostages go and we'll finish this? We can knock heads then. Clean. Quick. Man-to-man style. Or maybe you don't have the balls for that, Hammadi?"

How did this American know his name? Hammadi wondered. Bradley Milton, that was it. They had been hired to rescue the hostages by Milton—or had they? Were they some special so-called antiterrorist force? And how many were they? Hammadi, looking around at the torn and twisted bodies strewn across the compound, the corpses tangled in the barbwire to the east, decided flight was better now than to stay and fight. Tomorrow was another day. Tomorrow he would regroup, rebuild his force. He would be back. It was no longer a question of balls, Hammadi bitterly thought, feeling the sting of the American's insult. No, it was simply a question of survival.

"Dhourjan. Take some of the men with you. Go start up one of the trucks."

Quickly, Dhourjan, signaling a group of seven *Sadi* soldiers, moved away from the ammo depot.

"If one shot is fired, they all die! Do you understand me?"

"Don't be stupid, Hammadi!" Gabriel called back. "They die, you've got nothing to bargain with. They die, you die, too. What's it going to be?"

"Move, move!" Hammadi hissed at his soldiers. As they hustled the hostages away from the depot, Hammadi looked toward the GAZ-66 transport trucks.

Then he saw her.

Pamela Milton became a shadow as she moved away from the beam of the klieg light. Before she disappeared behind the barracks, Hammadi spotted the silvery backpack. The crazy bitch, he thought. *What's she going to do?*


Gabriel pulled the pin on the MK2 frag grenade. "Ready?" he asked Dillinger as the P.I., the .45 Colt tucked inside his belt, took the grenade.

"This is crazy!"

*I hear ya*, Gabriel thought. Yanking the pin out of his own MK2 grenade, releasing the spoon, he said, "There's no negotiating here, Zac. We're not exactly the UN, y'know."

Together, they hurled the grenades.

As the grenades bounced near the Arabs covered

behind the corners of the barracks, Gabriel crouched. His M16 on single-shot mode, he pumped a slug between the eyes of an Arab who was guarding the hostages.

Dillinger snaked the .45 Colt out of his belt.

Gabriel triggered his M203. The 40mm projectile streaked toward the ammo depot.

Hammadi shrieked a curse.

The .45 Colt boomed in Dillinger's hand.

An Arab skull shattered, the terrorist spinning away from his hostage.

The grenades blew, twin balls of fire launching bodies skyward.

A tremendous explosion roared thirty meters behind the hostages. As the hostages nose-dived to the earth, a whooshing geyser of flames lit the night.

Firing his M16 on the run, Gabriel cored a 5.56mm hole through an Arab's forehead as that Muslim triggered his Kalashnikov. Slugs whined off the stone beside Gabriel's head as he hugged the wall of the barracks.

The .45 Colt bucked twice in Dillinger's hand. Down-range, the P.I.'s Muslim target pitched backward as the slugs punched into his chest.

Swiftly, ramming a fresh thirty-round clip into his M16, switching the mode back to full-auto, Gabriel moved toward the hostages.

"I haven't seen the old man's wonder girl anywhere," Dillinger called out, covering Gabriel's backside, the .45 Colt fanning the area around the barracks.

And Gabriel didn't see any sign of Muhmad Hammadi, either.

"Where the hell are Johnny-Boy and the Dutchman?" Dillinger wondered aloud, as they neared the end of the barracks.

Reaching the hostages, Gabriel asked, "Anybody hurt?"

Four pairs of eyes that had seen a living hell looked up at Gabriel. Beside Gabriel, fire towered into the sky, turning night into day, it seemed, around the ex-CIA assassin. His face sheened by sweat, a wild look in his eyes, Gabriel peered at the hostages. Only four men. Then he remembered what one of the hostages had said during the standoff. One of them had been murdered. As the hostages stared at Gabriel, the bitter hatred in their eyes melted into relief, gratitude.

"Wh-who are you?" one of the hostages asked Gabriel.

"I'm an American. You're going home."

"Vic!"

The crackle of flames in his ears, Gabriel made out the voice of Boolewarke. MM-1 in hand, the Dutchman limped out of the flickering shadows to the north. Johnny Simms, searching the darkness for any enemies in hiding, covered the Dutchman's rear with his M16.

Engines rumbled to life behind Gabriel. The Russian transport trucks, he thought. Hammadi was beating a hasty retreat.

"Zac, Johnny! Get these men outta here. Meet us at the end of the barracks."

Firelight wavered over the Dutchman as he closed on Gabriel. "The Ivan trucks?"

"Yeah."

"Sounds like you got somethin' in mind for this MM-1."

"Fireworks, Dutch," Dillinger called out as the P.I. and Simms helped the hostages to their feet.

The GAZ-66 transport truck lumbered toward Gabriel and Boolewarke, the driver grinding the clutch.

An AK-47 flamed from the passenger window of the truck. Gabriel recognized the gunman as Hammadi.

Slugs tattooing the wall of the barracks above him, Gabriel hit a combat crouch.

Strung out in a ragged line down the side of the GAZ-66 transports, *Sadi* soldiers unleashed autofire at Boolewarke and Dillinger.

"I got the runaway!" Gabriel yelled, and triggered his M203.

Hammadi screamed a curse in Arabic.

Teeth gritted, Boolewarke unloaded the MM-1. Round after 38mm round streaked off into the darkness.

And darkness became lit by boiling explosions that meshed into one huge wave of fire. The sky seemed to open, swallow up flying wreckage as a line of fiery blasts pulverized the GAZ-66 transport trucks.

The rampaging Russian truck erupted, less than a hundred feet from Gabriel and Dillinger. Hammadi's expression of maniacal rage vanished inside the fiery cloud.

"Yaaaaaahhhh!!!" Boolewarke yelled in rage, as he emptied the twelve chambers of the squat launcher, debris skimming the ground in front of the Dutchman, twisted strips of metal razoring through the air.

Slowly, Gabriel stood. The fuel inside the transport trucks, ignited by the explosions, roared and roared, screaming through the night on giant tongues of fire. Nothing, Gabriel knew, could have survived that hell. The crackle of fire filled Gabriel's ears. He looked at Boolewarke, and read the fear in the Dutchman's eyes.

Instinctively, Gabriel flung himself to the ground. He heard the hiss, then, as the dragon's tongue of flames shot over him, he felt the heat scorch his back. Gabriel was afraid for Boolewarke, but since he didn't hear the bone-chilling screams of a man being burned alive, he rolled, came up, firing. Knowing he was a heartbeat away from being roasted alive, terror exploded the adrenaline through Gabriel's veins. As he triggered the M16, Gabriel discovered he'd found Pamela Milton. The tracking line of fire ripping into her chest, the woman spun. Screaming, she held back on the nozzle's trigger.

Fire roared down the length of the wall.

Boolewarke cut loose with his M16. Flames rushed at the Dutchman's face. A millisecond later, his stream of 5.56mm lead-jacketed hornets punched into the silver backpack, as Gabriel's swarm of bullets bounced Pamela Milton off the wall.

The ruptured backpack exploded.

But Pamela Milton was already dead.

"Jesus bloody Christ!" Boolewarke rasped.

Grimly, Gabriel watched as burning bits and pieces of Milton's daughter rained to the ground. Gabriel swallowed hard, felt his arm go limp as the M16 lowered by his side.

Boolewarke looked at Gabriel, his gaze narrowed. "Was that . . . "

"Yeah, Dutch. That was her. Milton's daughter."

"Jesus bloody Christ. What'll we tell the old man?"

"I don't know."

A numbing weariness settled over Gabriel. He felt as if he was a hundred years old.

# Chapter 14

"I'm not looking forward to this, at all," Johnny Simms said. "I got a feeling the old man's gonna flip out real bad."

Gabriel steered the Land Rover across the gravel plain. In the distance, he saw Milton's white Lear jet parked near the foothills of the Tébessa Mountains. There was no sign of Black Lightning.

Gabriel agreed with Simms. Bradley Milton wasn't going to greet Eagle Force with open arms.

Henry van Boolewarke slumped his head back, shut his eyes. The Dutchman had cleaned and bandaged his own wounds, then administered to Dillinger's wounds and shattered collarbone. The white-haired commando now had his right arm in a sling. One of the .45 Colts, Gabriel noticed, was tucked inside the top of Dillinger's pants, the pearl-handled butt jutting out for a crossdraw.

Trouble, right. Gabriel expected Milton was going to be enraged when he learned the whole ugly truth. But there was only one way to tell Milton. Point-blank. This was going to be one of the harder things he had done in a while. When family went bad or one of your own dies or, worse, is murdered, Gabriel thought . . . Christ. He felt all the old pain and rage coming on. Then he shut out the ghosts of terrible memories.

"At least the rest of the hostages are on their way back to the States," Boolewarke said. "We did something right anyway."

"And we cleaned North Africa of a human dungheap, don't forget that either, Dutch," Dillinger reminded the Afrikaaner.

Boolewarke grunted. "Cleaned? My white-haired friend, do you know how many more terrorists there are running amok in North Africa?"

Dillinger showed Boolewarke a mean smile. "You mean we got more body counts to take?"

"I don't know, maybe you, not me. I was thinking about collecting my money and going home," Boolewarke said and let out a breath.

One hand on the wheel, Gabriel flicked his engraved Zippo, fired up a Marlboro. "C'mon, Dutch. At the risk of sounding like a heartless bastard . . . you've got nothing to go back to."

Boolewarke clenched his jaw. "Don't you think I know that, Vic? Shit." He stared out the window. Harsh sunlight burned off the plain, and Gabriel saw the bright light glint against Boolewarke's eyes for a second. There was pain, bitter pain and hatred in the Dutchman's eyes.

Gabriel bled inside for the Dutchman. Life could be ugly, unfair, unjust. Every man paid a price somewhere down the road. And a man never stops paying dues. Dues either to the devil or . . .

"Y'know, man," Simms suddenly said to Boolewarke. "This whole thing's made me take a little harder look at myself . . . and . . ."

"Put a lid on it, Johnny-Boy," Boolewarke cut in. "I know what you're trying to say. No apologies. No excuses. What's done is done. Any feelings you got, one way or another, keep 'em to yourself."

"What I was trying to tell ya, stormtrooper," Simms growled, but with a note of humor in his voice, "is that for a South African shitkicker you ain't such a bad motherfucker. Even though you are a *bad* motherfucker."

A weary smile creased Boolewarke's lips. "You're not the first black merc I've seen who's knocked down the myth that blacks aren't worth a shit when it comes to soldiering, Johnny. I had my doubts about you. And you, too," the Dutchman told Dillinger. "You came through. Like real troopers." He cracked a grin. "Stormtroopers."

"Does that mean you're staying on, Dutch?" Gabriel wanted to know.

Boolewarke was silent for a long moment. "I don't know, Vic. I'll let you know something."

There was silence for several stretched seconds. The Land Rover closed down on the foothills. Gabriel took in the scene. For some reason, Gabriel felt as if he were driving to a funeral. Whose funeral, though? he wondered.

Milton and his three bodyguards were waiting near the Lear Jet. Radar, Gabriel thought, for bad news. On the floorboard beside Gabriel was the briefcase with the counterfeit money. He was going to give the briefcase back to Gabriel, then collect—or try to collect—what was due him. It was simply a question of what Milton would now think Eagle Force was due.

"If there ever was a such a thing as blood money," Simms commented, "we're collecting it."

"Do you think those hostages will talk?" Dillinger asked.

"I don't really care at this point, Zac," Gabriel answered. "They're going home, that's what matters. If they talk, they talk. They don't really know anything except that four ugly bastards who can roll like a juggernaut pulled their tails out of the fire."

"Yeah," Simms said. "But did we win or did we lose?"

Right. Gabriel wasn't sure. Time would tell.

And the time had come.

Gabriel braked, parked the Land Rover near Black Lightning. Killing the engine, Gabriel cocked the bolt on Little Lightning, holstered the mini-Uzi in his special shoulder holster. A thirty-round magazine, he hoped would be enough to finish the job if things got rough

Simms and Boolewarke cocked bolts on their mini-Uzis, too.

"Let's go," Gabriel said. Briefcase in hand, he opened the door, stepped out into the harsh sunlight.

Slowly, Eagle Force walked toward Milton and his bodyguards. Gabriel spotted a briefcase, similar to the one he was carrying, sitting on the ground beside Milton.

"Well?" Milton gruffed. "Where is she? Where's my daughter?"

The bodyguards unzipped their windbreakers, reached for their holstered Magnums.

"Don't do that!" Gabriel rasped, draping his hand over the mini-Uzi.

The bodyguards froze.

"I don't like what I'm seeing, Mr. Gabriel," Milton growled.

Eagle Force spread out. Dillinger and Simms flanked Gabriel's left, and Boolewarke stood off to the right of the ex-CIA assassin.

"Do you have our money, Mr. Milton?" Gabriel asked, a ball of sweat breaking from his brow, burning into his narrowed gaze.

Milton kicked at the briefcase. "I asked you a question."

"Is the money there?"

Milton jerked a nod at one of his bodyguards. The bodyguard opened the briefcase, showed a stack of bills to Gabriel.

"Now . . . answer my question."

"I'm afraid I have some bad news, Mr. Milton," Gabriel began. "Your daughter was one of them. Why, I can't tell you. I just don't know. Maybe you've got some answers to the mystery, Milton. Whatever . . . it's none of my business really."

Milton trembled with suppressed rage. "You're lying."

"She's dead, too."

"You fucking bastards!" Milton screamed. "What are you telling me?"

"The truth. I don't know how else I can tell you this. She was sleeping with one of them. You were set up."

"I don't believe you. Where is she?"

It was time to get ugly, Gabriel decided. "In about a million pieces spread across the *Sadi* compound. She turned on us. We blew her away."

"You rotten cocksuckers," Milton hissed. "I'll find out my goddamned self. And, if you're telling the truth, which I don't believe you are, you won't get one fucking dime from me."

"I'm telling you the truth right here, right now, Milton," Gabriel said, grim-faced. "Let's square the tab, all right? The Sword of Islam is finished. We fulfilled your contract."

Milton looked long and hard at Gabriel with bitter hatred in his eyes. Finally, he nodded.

"Fine, we'll square the tab, right here, right now," Milton said. "Maybe there's a chance you are telling the truth. If you are . . . well, I'll never have to lay eyes on you again." The mogul glanced at his bodyguards, then picked up the briefcase, walked toward his Lear jet.

"What's this, Milton?" Gabriel barked.

Then all hell broke loose.

The bodyguards clawed for leather.

"Shit! Crazy bastards!" Simms bellowed.

The .44 Magnums whipped from shoulder holsters.

Eagle Force moved like a wink of lightning.

The .45 Colt cannoned in Dillinger's fist.

Gabriel, Simms, and Boolewarke cut loose with the mini-Uzis as a .44 round thundered from the hand cannon of a bodyguard.

As quick as the bodyguards were, Eagle Force had just stepped out of the bowels of hell. They were in no mood to be fucked with.

Eagle Force beat the bodyguards to the draw.

Milton nose-dived to the ground.

Blood, flesh, and chunks of cloth were sheared away from the chests of the bodyguards as 9mm Parabellum slugs and .45 ACP rounds stitched their chests, kicked them back, pinning their twitching bodies against the fuselage of the Lear Jet. Blood washed over Milton's face.

As the corpses slid down the fuselage, trailing crimson streaks on the white paint job of the Lear jet, Milton swept up a .44 Magnum.

"Milton, don't do it!" Gabriel warned.

Milton didn't listen to the warning. He leapt to his feet, screaming a curse.

Bradley Milton III died.

Eagle Force crucified him to the fuselage of the Lear Jet, the mini-Uzis stuttering in the hands of Gabriel, Simms, and Boolewarke, the .45 Colt booming twice in Dillinger's fist.

Milton, jaw gaping, eyes squeezed shut, toppled to the earth, the .44 Magnum cannoning a round skyward.

The pilot swung into the fuselage doorway, drew down on Eagle Force with an M16. He died in a hellstorm of lead, as Eagle Force ventilated him with an extended fusillade. Jerking like a puppet on a string, the pilot bounced around in the doorway, thudded off the wing, and slammed to the ground.

Quickly, Simms and Boolewarke ran to the jet. Ramming home fresh thirty-round clips into their mini-Uzis, they flanked the doorway, burst inside, crouched, ready to fire.

Moments later, Simms told Gabriel, "Nothing."

"All right, take Milton's briefcase," Gabriel told Simms. "Get in the Land Rover."

Gabriel picked up the briefcase with the counterfeit money.

"What are you gonna do, Vic?" Dillinger asked, as Gabriel walked toward the jet.

"Finish a dead man's payoff."

Gabriel slung the briefcase through the fuselage doorway. Plucking an MK2 frag grenade off his webbing, he pulled the pin and pitched the grenade into the jet.

Gabriel ran.

The frag grenade detonated, puked out the fuselage of the Lear Jet in a fiery hail of twisted metal shards. Fuel ignited, and a giant fireball pulped the jet into scrap.

Wreckage pounded to the earth behind Gabriel.

For long moments, Eagle Force watched as the fire blazed a path away from the wreckage, incinerating the corpses.

Flaming shreds of money floated to the ground.

"Blood money, yeah," Johnny Simms said, tight-lipped. "Think any of this will come back to earth in one piece?"

*Right*, Gabriel sarcastically thought. *If it does, maybe some drifting Bedouin nomads will put it to good use and screw Uncle Sam some more. Maybe they'll take out stock in OPEC, and with their newfound wealth, they'll fight to bring down the price of oil in their generosity and compassion. Yeah. Right. And Muhammad will be there for the Second Coming.*

## COCAINE CARTEL!

The younger brother of Eagle Force leader
Vic Gabriel has just died from a cocaine overdose . . . and Vic is hot for revenge. Rather
than go after low-level drug dealers, Vic rounds
up the men of Eagle Force to smash the billion-
dollar coke cartel, run by the evil but cunning El
Diablo in a man-made hell called . . .

# DEATH CAMP
# COLOMBIA

Here's an exciting preview of Book #2
in Dan Schmidt's EAGLE FORCE series:
DEATH CAMP COLOMBIA!
*They're coming at you!*
Look for EAGLE FORCE
wherever Bantam Books are sold.

Fernando Cortes Hernandez was smiling. He had been dealt a setback, but he was back on the road to recovering his empire, and he would return to his throne, the gilded man. The smile vanishing, he rested a cheroot on his thin bloodless lips, snapped the 24-carat gold case shut and slipped the smokeholder inside his suit jacket. With a silver Ronson lighter he torched the cheroot, then ran well-manicured fingers over the lapel of his jacket, relished the exquisite cool touch of a thousand dollars' worth of Thai silk against his skin. He stared through the French double-doors. Beyond the lagoon, he saw the first golden rays of dawn jagging across the southern Florida sky. A pelican spread its wings and flapped over the lagoon. Six DEA agents, armed with assault rifles, patrolled the grounds beyond the ivy-trellised and palm-tree-fringed patio.

*Death was coming in the eye of dawn*, the man known as El Diablo thought, drawing the sweet cheroot smoke into his lungs. *And there will be fire in the sky*. The fire of the Devil.

Soon, El Diablo told himself, soon he would be a free man again. And the world would once more belong to him. The world and all its riches.

Death would bring him freedom. Shortly, he would get back to business as usual.

"Look at that guy, willya? Christ, the sight of him makes me sick. It's all I can do to keep from ripping his throat out with my bare hands."

Short but muscular, the swarthy, dark-haired Hernandez flexed his left hand, feeling the strength flow through his veins, his blood running hot with a burning hunger to be free. He wanted to laugh at the DEA agents. The tall, muscular agent named Stiles was losing badly at a game of spades. The shorter, heavyset Jameson chuckled each time he set his partner. Life was a game, after all, Hernandez decided. In his game, however, there were no winners—only survivors. And only one king of the mountain, one god of an empire that stretched around the world.

One conqueror.

Yes, Fernando Cortes Hernandez believed he was stronger, much, much stronger than any straight DEA man would ever be in a hundred lifetimes. Both physically and financially those agents of the DEA were impotent, he thought. They were men who dreamed of a drug-free world, dreamers, *sí*, who wanted to believe in the job they were doing. Blinded either by dreams, ambition, or their own smallness in a world they could never control, what they didn't want to see was that cocaine equalled big money.

Big, big *dinero*. The kind of money, Hernandez thought, and felt another tight grin stretch his lips, that God had. As long as politicians and law enforcement officers accepted a piece of the biggest action the world had ever seen, the world, and particularly *los Estados Unidos*, Fernando Cortes Hernandez knew, would never be drug-free. And he would keep on playing God.

Or the Devil. He was the one with the real power. The power of life and death.

"Relax, Big John. The Colombian's shit, we all know that. There's no sense getting your blood pressure pounding over him. I'd hate to see you have a heart attack right before the big day when we start to flush this piece of shit down the toilet. Besides," Jameson added, smiling, "you'd better get your mind back on this game of spades. At fifty cents a point, I'm up three hundred and twenty-five points."

They knew he could hear them, perhaps even wanted him to show anger over their barbs and cynical remarks. But they were as nothing to Fernando Cortes Hernandez. Indeed, they were less than the *campesinos* of his country. His cartel worth in excess of fifty billion dollars a year, worth far more than the 31.6 billion dollar GNP of his own country, Hernandez knew he could buy and sell them all a thousand times over. And if he couldn't buy and sell them like the dog meat they were, he thought, he could crush them like the worms they were.

"Look at this place, willya? A fancy mahogany bar in the corner of the room, loaded down with booze. A goddamn Jacuzzi in the living room. A stinkin' Olympic-sized pool out back. A bed with satin sheets for the drug-pushing shit. Cable television. We gotta keep the Colombian on ice in a palace that would make English royalty look like they were living in poverty."

"You know the routine, Big John," Hernandez heard Jameson sigh. "We've got to keep these hotshot Federal witnesses comfortable so they don't change their minds about singing. At least, that's the theory, anyway."

Hernandez kept smiling. He was used to style. And, he had to admit, the spacious, stone-and-marble mansion, secluded somewhere south of Miami, was indeed stylish. The DEA had broken their backs to make him comfortable. Then again, they had also broken their backs to extradite him from his ranchhouse outside of Medellin. Had he not been so burned out from four straight days of partying, the DEA men would never have caught him. Rule of thumb in the cocaine trade: Never get high on your own supply. But when a man is refining close to fifty tons of cocaine a month, he could afford to dip into his own supply, Hernandez thought. Hell, he could afford to shovel into the stuff.

"Only this snowbird may be snowing us about his big plea-bargaining routine," Stiles growled. "That Federal Witness Protection tag leaves a real bad taste in my mouth. For some reason, I got the feeling our boy here may just be buying time."

"For what?"

"I dunno. How should I know?"

Jameson smiled indulgently. "Take it easy, Big John. Remember, paranoia will destroy ya."

"Paranoia, huh? We've got twenty of our people and ten Miami vice cops toting M16s and submachine guns, assigned to protect the life of a cocaine vampire who calls himself the Devil," Stiles bitched. "And for what? So he can have his big day in a Miami court and walk away on some technicality? Plea-bargain his way back to Colombia? Maybe some judge who's got a nose-candy habit himself getting bought off by those big cocaine dollars? I'm not just paranoid, guy, I'm getting blind pissed-off just thinking about how these *coquitos* can twist, bend, and shit all over the system. And nobody seems to be able to do a damn thing about it. We nabbed him, sure, but the cocaine king is far from dead. If you ask me, all this beefed-up security may just be a sore thumb looking to get hacked off. And we're that thumb. Look at 'im," he said, jaw clenched, eyes burning at Hernandez. "Federal witness, my ass. Big songbird. Bullshit."

Jameson sighed. "How many death threats have been issued against our people this last week? Death threats that have been carried out, I'll remind you. Our agents overseas have been practically under siege since our people bagged and extradited Hernandez from Colombia," Jameson said. "Three agents shotgunned to death then hacked up in the street of Bogotá—a street full of witnesses, but nobody saw or heard a damn thing. Four more submachine-gunned in Bolivia. An agent in Panama shipped back to D.C. in bits and pieces. Now the hellstorm's blowing right across our own backyard—the family of a vice cop kidnapped and tortured to death right here in Miami."

"And you can bet we've got the sonofabitch behind it all," Stiles replied. "Right here, grinning from ear to ear, in our faces. Like he knows something we don't. I tell ya, either he bullshitted us about testifying or somebody down there is scared he might start pointing fingers to save his own skin."

Blowing smoke, Hernandez turned away from the French double doors. "You have a big mouth, *hombre*."

"What's that?" Stiles growled, and suddenly draped his hand over the stock of his M16. "You say something, shithead?"

"Relax, for chrissakes, will ya, John?" Jameson implored. "Get your hand off that M16 before you do something stupid."

"Stupid." Hernandez chuckled, then looked away from Stiles's burning gaze. "Stupid, perhaps. Bitter, *sí*. Simple, *sí*. Yours is a simple job for a simple mind. A simple man is often a bitter man, too. Simple life. Bitter ways. Dead-end life."

"I don't see how you quite figure all that

garbage about dead ends, Hernandez," Stiles said, his voice edged with anger. "You're the one who got caught with your lips locked on a crack pipe and dragged out of Colombia."

"The world," Hernandez said, solemnly gazing at the guards near the patio, "is a whore, and you must indulge her. The sooner you learn that . . . the better off you'll be."

Stiles grinned at Jameson. "The world's a whore? Now what's that—"

Suddenly, the DEA agents froze, locked gazes. The cards slipped out of Stiles's hand.

The throbbing seemed to descend right on top of the safe house.

"Are we expecting company?" Stiles rasped, snatching up his M16. "That's a chopper! Nobody told me anything—"

The sounds of autofire, screams lanced through the windows of the room.

Looking skyward, Hernandez smiled, his eyes lit with grim anticipation. He flicked his cheroot aside as the French Aerospatiale Alouette swooped from the murky sky. A split second later, as the DEA agents opened up on the converted gunship with a barrage of M16 autofire, the chopper turned the stygian gloom ablaze.

Fire ripped the dawn sky asunder.

A glowing tongue of white phosphorous fire spewed from the long nozzle on the gunship's nose. Shrieks ripped the air, and M16s went silent as the DEA agents burst into human torches. Flaming demons crashed through the trellis, wrapped in slick-looking sheets of fire. A wave of flames consumed the patio, devouring plants and human life alike.

A demon danced in front of the French double doors. Flailing, he tumbled through those doors, wailing like a banshee. Glass shards razored past Hernandez, who held his ground. Silently, he dared the fickle gods of fate to hurt him.

"Jesus Christ!" Stiles gasped, freezing in his tracks for a second, his face cut with horror and shock as the blood curdling screams filled the room. "We're being hit! What the hell's—"

Hernandez then saw the dark shadows pouring out of the woods. Automatic weapons chattered in their fists, spewing hot lead over the stunned DEA agents.

"You sonofabitch! You planned this whole thing! You set us up!"

Hernandez whirled. There was murderous rage in Stiles's eyes. For a moment, the cocaine czar would have sworn that Stiles was going to cut him down in cold blood.

"John! John!"

The demon's screams died. The stench of roasting flesh pierced Hernandez's nose. It was a good smell, he thought. The cleansing fire. The corpse was the charred, shriveled symbol of the moral decay of the United States.

Then Hernandez saw the pencil-tip flame spitting from the muzzle of Jameson's M16.

Stiles cried out, a line of 5.56mm slugs marching up the backs of his legs. As Stiles crumpled to the floor, Hernandez scooped up the fallen M16. For a stretched second, Hernandez and Jameson stared at each other.

Teeth gnashing, Stiles grabbed at his legs, rolling around in a growing puddle of his own blood.

Hernandez smiled at Jameson. The furious din of autofire crushed in on the safe house.

"So I am a piece of *mierda*, eh, *hombre?*"

Jameson shrugged, appearing apologetic. "C'mon, give me a break. I had to make it sound convincing."

"No . . . no." Stiles looked up at Jameson, his eyes burning with hatred. "Not you. Not—"

"Finish him, *hombre.*"

Regret flashed through Jameson's eyes. He looked down at Stiles. "Sorry, Big John. What can I tell you? I got caught in a tangled web."

Without hesitation, Jameson drilled a 3-round burst into Stiles's chest.

The gunship lowered to the ground beyond the shattered French double doors. Rotor wash hurled chips of glass against Hernandez. His gaze narrowed against the glass shrapnel, Hernandez told Jameson, "Your information had better be good, *hombre.* Or you will not live to see the sun set. *Comprende?*"

The smoking M16 was lowered to Jameson's side. "It's good. I wouldn't risk my ass like this if it weren't."

Hernandez grunted.

There was a commotion behind Jameson.

Three swarthy men surged through the

doorway. With long strides, Hernandez moved toward his soldiers. They toted Argentine FMK-3 submachine guns. Hernandez smiled. There was no mistaking his *segundo* and top assassin, Raul El Leon Pizarro. Six and a half feet tall, with shoulder-length hair as black as coal and an eyepatch over his left eye, Pizarro, Hernandez knew, could put fear into the heart of the toughest of *hombres*. There was a huge machete sheathed in black leather at Pizarro's side. More than once, Hernandez had seen El Leon hack the arms or legs off an enemy and feed the bloody stump to a caiman.

"Fernando," Pizarro greeted, and the two men hugged each other. "I knew we would see each other again."

"Once again, Raul, you have shown you have the courage of a lion."

"They were nothing. The place is surrounded. All of the DEA men are dead. Another helicopter is on the way now to lift us out."

"Good, good. We must leave now. Quickly."

Suspiciously, Pizarro looked at Jameson. "Wait a minute, Fernando. What about him?"

"Him? Do not forget—that *gringo* has the masterlist, Raul. He lives . . . for now." A cruel smile then stretched the cocaine czar's lips as he looked at the body of Stiles. "Let us see, though, if he has the stomach for what may lie ahead in the days to come for his DEA *amigos*. Give our new addition to the New Conquistadors your machete, Raul."

Jameson tensed, as Pizarro slid the machete from its sheath. "Wh-what . . ."

"Be quick about it, *hombre*," Hernandez snapped at Jameson. "Raul, you watch him and make sure he does admirable work. If he hesitates, kill him. Sometimes they vomit over such work. Should he vomit, kill him."

Jameson looked at the machete as if it were some contagious virus.

"Take it!" Hernandez barked.

Trembling, Jameson took the machete. "Wh-what . . . what do you want me to do with it?"

Hernandez smiled. "You are to make Big John not so big, *hombre*, that's what."

El Diablo laughed.

It was back to business as usual.

The statistics were frightening.

The newspaper headlines were horrifying.

The world had gone mad.

Vic Gabriel felt his teeth set on edge. Expelling a pent-up breath, he looked up from the *Washington Post*. Beneath Gabriel was a glaring headline about the massacre of DEA agents and Miami vice detectives at a safe house in Dade County, a hit that had gone down because of the extradition of a drug baron from Colombia. Another major supplier of cocaine, who had also been extradited recently from Colombia, had been quoted in the article Gabriel had just read: *Cocaine will be the atom bomb that destroys the United States*.

The sonofabitch had that right, Gabriel thought, and felt the bitterness eating away at his guts.

Cocaine had killed his younger brother, Jim, years ago.

Following his brother's death, Vic Gabriel had launched a short but explosive war against the death pushers, up and down the East Coast. During that war, Gabriel had found a close ally within the Drug Enforcement Administration. That agent, Bob Jeffreys, had sympathized with Gabriel and put his job, and his life, on the line for the man in the belief that fire had to be fought with fire. For days now, Gabriel had been poring over and mentally chewing up the intelligence Jeffreys had air-expressed to him from across the Atlantic Ocean. The statistics were enough to send someone reeling in disbelief. More than two billion dollars of cocaine was squeezed into Florida alone every week. And that, according to the agent's intel, was a conservative estimate . . . a very conservative estimate. It was reported that only one in every nine hauls of cocaine was seized by law enforcement officials. Tons of cocaine were stockpiled in refineries in Colombia, Bolivia, Peru, and other South American countries. Plenty of the black snow, Gabriel thought, to replace any load that was confiscated. The DEA and other law enforcement agencies simply didn't have the manpower or the money to win the war against the *narcotraficantes*. It was the drug barons who had all the money, all the manpower. And they never hesitated to flex muscle when and wherever necessary to get what they wanted.

Shaking a Marlboro free from a rumpled pack, Gabriel flicked a gold-plated Zippo, torched the smoke. Engraved on the Zippo was *7th SFG— No compromise*. The Zippo was a memento from his father, Colonel Charles Gabriel, who had helped in the conception of the Special Forces in 1952.

Vic Gabriel himself was ex–Special Forces. He was also a former assassin for the CIA's Special Operations Division. It was because of the CIA that Vic Gabriel and the other three commandos of Eagle Force were forced to set up a new base of operations in the Pyrenees along the French-Spanish border. Eagle Force's last mission, a killhunt against the Soviet SPETSNAZ up the icy slopes of Mount Makalu in Nepal, had also locked them in the death sights of a CIA execution squad. After that mission, Eagle Force had wiped out the rest of that Company hit team in the Florida Everglades. Used as expendables by the CIA for a mission that had resulted in failure in Nepal, Eagle Force knew that the CIA would never give up the hunt to terminate them now. With the large sum of money they had managed to stash in a Swiss bank account after their first mission, the commandos of Eagle Force had bought out and set up their war base in a château, high up in the Pyrenees. Like any number of the ten thousand other châteaus in France, Gabriel's war base was originally built back in the Dark Ages to protect landowners from the barbarian hordes of Franks, Visigoths, and Burgundians. Vic Gabriel found grim irony in that. He knew there was really no safe place, no protection anywhere in the world from the savage hordes of animal man.